Max Brand

By

Alcatraz

1922

The Echo Library 2006

Published by

The Echo Library

Echo Library
131 High St.
Teddington
Middlesex TW11 8HH

www.echo-library.com

Please report serious faults in the text to complaints@echo-library.com

ISBN 1-84702-863-2

CONTENT

CHAPTER

CHAPTER I
CORDOVA

THE west wind came over the Eagles, gathered purity from the evergreen slopes of the mountains, blew across the foothills and league wide fields, and came at length to the stallion with a touch of coolness and enchanting scents of far-off things. Just as his head went up, just as the breeze lifted mane and tail, Marianne Jordan halted her pony and drew in her breath with pleasure. For she had caught from the chestnut in the corral one flash of perfection and those far-seeing eyes called to mind the Arab belief.

Says the Sheik: "I have raised my mare from a foal, and out of love for me she will lay down her life; but when I come out to her in the morning, when I feed her and give her water, she still looks beyond me and across the desert. She is waiting for the coming of a real man, she is waiting for the coming of a true master out of the horizon!"

Marianne had known thoroughbreds since she was a child and after coming West she had become acquainted with mere "hoss-flesh," but today for the first time she felt that the horse is not meant by nature to be the servant of man but that its speed is meant to ensure it sacred freedom. A moment later she was wondering how the thought had come to her. That glimpse of equine perfection had been an illusion built of spirit and attitude; when the head of the stallion fell she saw the daylight truth: that this was either the wreck of a young horse or the sad ruin of a fine animal now grown old. He was a ragged creature with dull eyes and pendulous lip. No comb had been among the tangles of mane and tail for an unknown period; no brush had smoothed his coat. It was once a rich red-chestnut, no doubt, but now it was sun-faded to the color of sand. He was thin. The unfleshed backbone and withers stood up painfully and she counted the ribs one by one. Yet his body was not so broken as his spirit. His drooped head gave him the appearance of searching for a spot to lie down. He seemed to have been left here by the cruelty of his owner to starve and die in the white heat of this corral—a desertion which he accepted as justice because he was useless in the world.

It affected Marianne like the resignation of a man; indeed there was more personality in the chestnut than in many human beings. Once he had been a beauty, and the perfection which first startled her had been a ghost out of his past. His head, where age or famine showed least, was still unquestionably fine. The ears were short and delicately made, the eyes well-placed, the distance to the angle of the jaw long—in brief, it was that short head of small volume and large brain space which speaks most eloquently of hot blood. As her expert eye ran over the rest of the body she sighed to think that such a creature had come to such an end. There was about him no sign of life save the twitch of his skin to shake off flies.

Certainly this could not be the horse she had been advised to see and she was about to pass on when she felt eyes watching her from the steep shadow of the shed which bordered the corral. Then she made out a dapper olive-skinned fellow sitting with his back against the wall in such a position of complete relaxation as only a Mexican is capable of assuming. He wore a short tuft of black moustache cut well away from the edge of the red lip, a moustache which oddly accentuated his youth. In body and features he was of that feminine delicacy which your large-handed Saxon dislikes, and though Marianne was by no means a stalwart, she detested the man at once. For that reason, being a lady to the tips of her slim fingers, her smile was more cordial than necessary.

"I am looking for Manuel Cordova," she said.

"Me," replied the Mexican, and managed to speak without removing the cigarette.

"I'm glad to know you." she answered. "I am Marianne Jordan."

At this, Manuel Cordova removed his cigarette, regardless of the ashes which tumbled straightway down the bell-mouthed sleeve of his jacket; for a Mexican deems it highly indecorous to pay the slightest heed to his tobacco ashes. Whether they land on chin or waistcoat they are allowed to remain until the wind carries them away.

"The pleasure is to me," said Cordova melodiously, and made painful preparations to rise.

She gathered at once that the effort would spoil his morning and urged him to remain where he was, at which he smiled with the care of a movie star, presenting an even, white line of teeth.

Marianne went on: "Let me explain. I've come to the Glosterville fair to buy some brood mares for my ranch and of course the ones I want are the Coles horses. You've seen them?"

He nodded.

"But those horses," she continued, checking off her points, "will not be offered for sale until after the race this afternoon. They're all entered and they are sure to win. There's nothing to touch them and when they breeze across the finish I imagine every ranch owner present will want to bid for them. That would put them above my reach and I can only pray that the miracle will happen—a horse may turn up to beat them. I made inquiries and I was told that the best prospect was Manuel Cordova's Alcatraz. So I've come with high hopes, Señor Cordova, and I'll appreciate it greatly if you'll let me see your champion."

"Look till the heart is content, señorita," replied the Mexican, and he extended a slim, lazy hand towards the drowsing stallion.

"But," cried the girl, "I was told of a real runner—"

She squinted critically at the faded chestnut. She had been told of a four-year-old while this gaunt animal looked fifteen at least. However, it is one thing to catch a general impression and another to read points. Marianne took heed, now, of the long slope of the shoulders, the short back, the well-let-down hocks. After all, underfeeding would dull the eye and give the ragged, lifeless coat.

"He is not much horse, eh?" purred Cordova.

But the longer she looked the more she saw. The very leanness of Alcatraz made it easier to trace his running-muscles; she estimated, too, the ample girth at the cinches where size means wind.

"And that's Alcatraz?" she murmured.

"That is all," said the pleasant Cordova.

"May I go into the corral and look him over at close range? I never feel that I know a horse till I get my hands on it."

She was about to dismount when she saw that the Mexican was hesitating and she settled back in the saddle, flushed with displeasure.

"No," said Cordova, "that would not be good. You will see!"

He smiled again and rising, he sauntered to the fence and turned about with his shoulders resting against the upper bar, his back to the stallion. As he did so, Alcatraz put forward his ears, which, in connection with the dullness of his eyes, gave him a peculiarly foolish look.

"You will see a thing, señorita!" the Mexican was chuckling.

It came without warning. Alcatraz turned with the speed of a whiplash curling and drove straight at the place where his master leaned. Marianne's cry of alarm was not needed. Cordova had already started, but even so he barely escaped. The chestnut on braced legs skidded to the fence, his teeth snapping short inches from the back of his master. His failure maddened Alcatraz. He reminded Marianne of the antics of a cat when in her play with the mouse she tosses her victim a little too far away and wheels to find her prospective meal disappearing down a hole. In exactly similar wise the stallion went around the corral in a whirl of dust, rearing, lashing out with hind legs and striking with fore, catching imaginary things in his teeth and shaking them to pieces. When the fury diminished he began to glide up and down the fence, and there was something so feline in the grace of those long steps and the intentness with which the brute watched Cordova that the girl remembered a new-brought tiger in the zoo. Also, rage had poured him full of such strength that through the dust cloud she caught again glimpses of that first perfection.

He came at last to a stop, but he faced his owner with a look of steady hate. The latter returned the gaze with interest, stroking his face and snarling: "Once more, red devil, eh? Once more you miss? Bah! But I, I shall not miss!"

It was not as one will talk to a dumb beast, for there was no mistaking the vicious earnestness of Cordova, and now the girl made out that he was caressing a long, white scar which ran from his temple across the cheekbone. Marianne glanced away, embarrassed, as people are when another reveals a dark and hidden portion of his character.

"You see?" said Cordova, "you would not be happy in the corral with him, eh?"

He rolled a cigarette with smiling lips as he spoke, but all the time his black eyes burned at the chestnut. He seemed to Marianne half child and half old man, and both parts of him were evil now that she could guess the whole story. Cordova campaigned through the country, racing his horse at fairs or for side bets. For two reasons he kept the animal systematically undernourished: one was that he was thereby able to get better odds; the other was that only on a weakened Alcatraz would he trust himself. At this she did not wonder for never had she seen such almost human viciousness of temper in a dumb beast.

"As for running, señorita," continued Cordova, "sometimes he does very well—yes, very well. But when he is dull the spurs are nothing to him."

He indicated a criss-crossing of scars on the flank of the stallion and Marianne, biting her lips, realized that she must leave at once if she wished to avoid showing her contempt, and her anger.

She was a mile down the road and entering the main street of Glosterville before her temper cooled. She decided that it was best to forget both Alcatraz and his master: they were equally matched in devilishness. Her last hope of seeing the mares beaten was gone, and with it all chance of buying them at a reasonable figure; for no matter what the potentialities of Alcatraz in his present starved condition he could not compare with the bays. She thought of Lady Mary with the sunlight rippling over her shoulder muscles. Certainly Alcatraz would never come within whisking distance of her tail!

CHAPTER II
THE COMING OF DAVID

HAVING reached this conclusion, the logical thing, of course, was for Marianne to pack and go without waiting to see the race or hear the bidding for the Coles horses; but she could not leave. Hope is as blind as love. She had left the ranch saying to her father and to the foreman, Lew Hervey: "The bank account is shrinking, but ideals are worth more than facts and I *shall* improve the horses on this place." It was a rather too philosophical speech for one of her years, but Oliver Jordan had merely shrugged his shoulders and rolled another cigarette; the crushed leg which, for the past three years, had made him a cripple, had taught him patience.

Only the foreman had ventured to smile openly. It was no secret that Lew Hervey disliked the girl heartily. The fall of the horse which made Jordan a semi-invalid, killed his ambition and self-reliance at the same instant. Not only was it impossible for him to ride since the accident, but the freeswinging self-confidence which had made him prosperous disappeared at the same time; his very thoughts walked slowly on foot since his fall. Hervey gathered the reins of the ranch affairs more and more into his own hands and had grown to an almost independent power when Marianne came home from school. Having studied music and modern languages, who could have suspected in Marianne either the desire or the will to manage a ranch, but to Marianne the necessity for following the course she took was as plain as the palm of an open hand. The big estate, once such a money-maker, was now losing. Her father had lost his grip and could not manage his own affairs, but who had ever heard of a hired man being called to run the Jordan business as long as there was a Jordan alive? She, Marianne, was very much alive. She came West and took the ranch in hand.

Her father smiled and gave her whatever authority she required; in a week the estate was hers to control. But for all her determination and confidence, she knew that she could not master cattle-raising in a few weeks. She was unfemininely willing to take advice. She even hunted for it, and though her father refused to enter into the thing even with suggestions, a little help from Hervey plus her indomitable energy might have made her attempt a success.

Hervey, however, was by no means willing to help. In fact, he was profoundly disgruntled. He had found himself, beyond all expectation, in a position almost as absolute and dignified as that of a real owner with not the slightest interference from Jordan, when on a sudden the arrival of this pretty little dark-eyed girl submerged him again in his old role of the hired man. He took what Marianne considered a sneaking revenge. He entered at once upon a career of the most perfect subordination. No fault could be found with his work. He executed every commission with scrupulous care. But when his advice was asked he became a sphinx. "Some folks say one way and some another. Speaking personal, I dunno, Miss Jordan. You just tell me what to do and I'll do it."

This attitude irritated her so that she was several times on the verge of discharging him, but how could she turn out so old an employee and one so painstaking in the duties assigned to him? Many a day she prayed for "a new foreman or night," but Hervey kept his job, and in spite of her best efforts, affairs went from bad to worse and the more desperately she struggled the more hopelessly she was lost. This affair of the horses was typical. No doubt the saddle stock were in sad need of improved blood but this was hardly the moment to undertake such an expenditure. Having once suggested the move, the quiet smiles of Hervey had spurred her on. She knew the meaning of those smiles. He was waiting till she should exhaust even the immense tolerance of her father; when she fell he would swing again into the saddle of control. Yet she would go on and buy the mares if she could. Hers was one of those militant spirits which, once committed, fights to the end along every line. And indeed, if she ever contemplated surrender, if she were more than once on the verge of giving way to the tears of broken spirit, the vague, uninterested eyes of her father and the overwise smiles of Hervey were whips which sent her back into the battle.

But today, when she regained her room in the hotel, she walked up and down with the feeling that she was struggling against manifest destiny. And in a rare burst of self-pity, she paused in front of the window, gritting her teeth to restrain a flood of tears.

A cowpuncher rocked across the blur of her vision on his pony, halted, and swung down in front of the stable across the street. The horse staggered as the weight came out of the stirrup and that made Marianne watch with a keener interest, for she had seen a great deal of merciless riding since she came West and it always angered her. The cowpunchers used "hoss-flesh" rather than horses, a distinction that made her hot. If a horse were not good enough to be loved it was not good enough to be ridden. That was one of her maxims. She stepped closer to the window. Certainly that pony had been cruelly handled for the little grey gelding swayed in rhythm with his panting; from his belly sweat dripped steadily into the dust and the reins had chafed his neck to a lather. Marianne flashed into indignation and that, of course, made her scrutinize the rider more narrowly. He was perfect of that type of cowboy which she detested most: handsome, lithe, childishly vain in his dress. About his sombrero ran a heavy width of gold-braid; his shirt was blue silk; his bandana was red; his boots were shop-made beauties, soft and flexible; and on his heels glittered—*gilded spurs!*

"And I'll wager," thought the indignant Marianne, "that he hasn't ten dollars in the world!"

He unknotted the cinches and drew off the saddle, propping it against one hip while he surveyed his mount. In spite of all his vainglory he was human enough to show some concern, it appeared. He called for a bucket of water and offered it to the dripping pony. Marianne repressed a cry of warning: a drink might ruin a horse as hot as that. But the gay rider permitted only a swallow and then removed the bucket from the reaching nose.

The old man who apparently sat all day and every day beside the door of the stable, only shifting from time to time to keep in shadow, passed his beard through his fist and spoke. Every sound, even of the panting horse, came clearly to her through the open window.

"Kind of small but kind of trim, that hoss."

"Not so small," said the rider. "About fifteen two, I guess."

"Measured him?"

"Never."

"I'd say nigher onto fifteen one."

"Bet my spurs to ten dollars that he's fifteen two; and that's good odds for you."

The old man hesitated; but the stable boy was watching him with a grin.

"I'll take that bet if—" he began.

The rider snapped him up so quickly that Marianne was angered again. Of course he knew the height of his own horse and it would be criminal to take the old loafer's money, but that was his determination.

"Get a tape, son. We'll see."

The stable boy disappeared in the shadow of the door and came back at once with the measure. The grey gelding, in the meantime, had smelled the sweetness of hay and was growing restive but a sharp word from the rider jerked him up like a tug on his bit. He tossed his head and waited, his ears flat.

"Look out, Dad," called the rider, as he arranged the tape to fall from the withers of the horse, "this little devil'll kick your head off quicker than a wink if he gets a chance."

"He don't look mean," said the greybeard, stepping back in haste.

"I like 'em mean and I keep 'em mean," said the other. "A tame hoss is like a tame man and I don't give a damn for a gent who won't fight."

Marianne covertly stamped. It was so easy to convert her worries into anger at another that she was beginning to hate this brutal-minded Beau Brummel of the ranges. Besides, she had had bitter experience with these noisy, careless fellows when they worked on her ranch. Her foreman was such a type grown to middle-age. Indeed her anger at the whole species called "cowpuncher" now focused to a burning-point on him of the gilded spurs.

The measuring was finished; he stepped back.

"Fifteen one and a quarter," he announced. "You win, Dad!"

Marianne wanted to cheer.

"You win, confound it! And where'll I get the mates of this pair? You win and I'm the underdog."

"A poor loser, too," thought Marianne. She was beginning to round her conception of the man; and everything she added to the picture made her dislike him the more cordially.

He had dropped on one knee in the dust and was busily loosening the spurs, paying no attention to the faint protests of the winner that he "didn't have no use for the darned things no ways." And finally he drowned the protests by breaking into song in a wide-ringing baritone and tossing the spurs at the feet of the others. He rose—laughing—and Marianne, with a mental wrest, rearranged one part of her preconception, yet this carelessness was only another form of the curse of the West and Westerners—extravagance.

He turned now to a tousle-headed three-year-old boy who was wandering near, drawn by the brilliance of the stranger.

"Keep away from those heels, kiddie. Look out, now!"

The yellow-haired boy, however, dazed by this sudden centering of attention on him, stared up at the speaker with his thumb in his mouth; and with great, frightened eyes—he headed straight for the heels of the grey!

"Take the hoss—" began the rider to the stable-boy. But the stable-boy's sudden reaching for the reins made the grey toss its head and lurch back towards the child. Marianne caught her breath as the stranger, with mouth drawn to a thin, grim line, leaped for the youngster. The grey lashed out with vicious haste, but that very haste spoiled his aim. His heels whipped over the shoulder of his master as the latter scooped up the child and sprang away. Marianne, grown sick, steadied herself against the side of the window; she had seen the brightness of steel on the driving hoofs.

A hasty group formed. The stable boy was guiltily leading the horse through the door and around the gaudy rider came the old man, and a woman who had run from a neighboring porch, and a long-moustached giant. But all that Marianne distinctly saw was the white, set face of the rescuer as he soothed the child in his arms; in a moment it had stopped crying and the woman received it. It was the old man who uttered the thought of Marianne.

"That was cool, young feller, and darned quick, and a nervy thing as I ever seen."

"Tut!" said the other, but the girl thought that his smile was a little forced. He must have heard those metal-armed hoofs as they whirred past his head.

"There is distinctly something worth while about these Westerners, after all," thought Marianne.

Something else was happening now. The big man with the sandy, long moustaches was lecturing him of the gay attire.

"Nervy enough," he began, "but you'd oughtn't to take a hoss around where kids are, a hoss that ain't learned to stop kicking. It's a fool thing to do, I say. I seen once where—"

He stopped, agape on his next word, for the lectured had turned on the lecturer, dropped his hands on his hips, and broke into loud laughter.

"Excuse me for laughing," he said when he could speak, "but I didn't see you before and—those whiskers, partner—those whiskers are—"

The laughter came again, a gale of it, and Marianne found herself smiling in sympathy. For they *were* odd whiskers, to be sure. They hung straight past the corners of the mouth and then curved sabre-like out from the chin. The sabre parts now wagged back and forth, as their owner moved his lips over words that would not come. When speech did break out it was a raging torrent that made Marianne stop her ears with a shiver.

Looking down the street away from the storming giant and the laughing cowpuncher, she saw that other folk had come out to watch, Westernlike. An

Eastern crowd would swiftly hem the enemies in a close circle and cheer them on to battle; but these Westerners would as soon see far off as close at hand. The most violent expression she saw was the broad grin of the blacksmith. He was a fine specimen of laboring manhood, that blacksmith, with the sun glistening on his sweaty bald head and over his ample, soot-darkened arms. Beside his daily work of molding iron with heat and hammer-blows, a fight between men was play; and now, with his hands on his hips, his manner was that of one relaxed in mood and ready for entertainment.

Presently he cast up his right arm and swayed to the left; then back; then rocked forward on his toes presenting two huge fists red with iron-rust and oil. It seemed that he was engaging in battle with some airy figure before him.

That was enough of a hint to make Marianne look again towards the pair directly below her; the hat of the gaudy cowpuncher lay in the dust where it had evidently been knocked by the first poorly aimed blow of him of the moustaches, and the owner of the hat danced away at a little distance. Marianne saw what the hat had hitherto concealed, a shock of flame-red hair, and she removed her fingers from her ears in time to hear the big man roar: "This ain't a dance, damn you! Stand still and fight!"

"Nope," laughed the other. "It ain't a dance. It's a pile more fun. Come on you—"

The big man obscured the last of the insulting description of his ancestry with the rush of a bull, his head lowered and his fists doing duty as horns. Plainly the giant had only to get one blow home to end the conflict, but swift and graceful as a tongue of fire dancing along a log the red-headed man flashed to one side, and as he whirled Marianne saw that he was laughing still, drunk with the joy of battle. Goliath roared past, thrashing the air; David swayed in with darting fists. They closed. They became obscure forms whirling in a fog of dust until red-head leaped out of the mist.

Goliath followed with the cloud boiling away from him, a mountain of a man above his foeman.

"It's unfair!" shrilled Marianne. "That great brute and—"

Red-head darted forward, a blue clad arm flicked out. She almost heard and felt the jar of that astonishing shock which halted Goliath in his tracks with one foot raised. He wobbled an instant, then his great knees bent, and dropping inert on his face the dust spurted like steam under the impact.

The crowd now washed in from every side to lift him up and revive him with canteens of water, yet they were quite jovial in the midst of their work of mercy and Marianne gathered that the fall of Goliath was not altogether unwelcome to the townsmen. She saw the bulky figure raised to a sitting posture, saw a dull-eyed face, bloody about the mouth, and looked away hastily towards the red-headed victor.

He was in the act of picking the torn fragments of his sombrero from the dust. It had probably come in contact with the giant's spurs as they wrestled, for the crown was literally ripped to tatters. And when its owner beat out the dirt and placed the hat on his head, the fiery hair was still visible through the rents.

Yet he was not downhearted, it seemed. He leaned jauntily against a hitching post under her window and rolled a cigarette, quite withdrawn from the crowd which was working over his victim.

Marianne began to feel that all she had seen was an ordinary chapter in his life; yet in the mere crossing of that street he had lost his spurs on a bet; saved a youngster from death at the risk of his own head, battled with a monster and now rolled a cigarette cheerily complacent. If fifty feet of his life made such a story what must a year of it be?

As though he felt her wonder above him, he raised his head in the act of lighting his cigarette and Marianne was looking down into bright, whimsical blue eyes. She was utterly unconscious of it at the moment but at the sight of that happy face and all the dust-dimmed finery of the cavalier, Marianne involuntarily smiled. She knew what she had done the moment he grinned in response and began to whistle, and whistle he did, keeping the rhythm with the sway of his head:

"At the end of the trail I'll be weary riding
But Mary will wait with a smile at the door;
The spurs and the bit had been chinking and chiding
But the end of the trail—"

Marianne stepped back from the window with the blood tingling in her face. She was terribly ashamed, for some reason, because she knew the words of that song.

"A cowpuncher—actually *whistling* at me!" she muttered, "I've never known a red-headed man who wasn't insolent!"

The whistling died out, a clear-ringing baritone began a new air:

"Oh, father, father William, I've seen your daughter dear.
Will you trade her for the brindled cow and the yellow steer?
And I'll throw in my riding boots and...."

Marianne slammed down the window. A moment later she was horrified to find herself smiling.

CHAPTER III
CONCERNING FIGHTERS

THE race-track had come into existence by grace of accident for it happened that a lane ran a ragged course about a big field taking the corners without pretense of making true curves, with almost an elbow-turn into the straightaway; but since the total distance around was over a mile it was called the "track." The sprints were run on the straightaway which was more than the necessary quarter of a mile but occasionally there was a longer race and then the field had to take that dangerous circuit, sloppy and slippery with dust. The land enclosed was used for the bucking contest, for the two crowning events of the Glosterville fiesta, the race and the horse-breaking, had been saved for this last day. Marianne Jordan gladly would have missed the latter event. "Because it sickens me to see a man fight with a horse," she often explained. But she forced herself to go.

She was in the Rocky Mountains, now, not on the Blue Grass. Here riding bucking horses was the order of the day. It might be rough, but this was a rough country.

It was a day of undue humidity—and the Eagle Mountains were pyramids of blue smoke. Closer at hand the roofs of Glosterville shone in the fierce sun and between the village and the mountains the open fields shimmered with rising heat waves. A hardy landscape meant only for a hardy people.

"One can't adopt a country," thought Marianne, "it's the country that does the adopting. If I'm not pleased by what pleases other people in the West, I'd better leave the ranch to Lew Hervey and go back East."

This was extraordinarily straight-from-the-shoulder thinking but all the way out to the scene of the festivities she pondered quietly. The episode of the mares was growing in importance. So far she had been able to do nothing of importance on the ranch; if this scheme fell through also it would be the proverbial last straw.

In spite of her intentions, she had delayed so long that the riding was very nearly ended before she arrived. Buckboards and automobiles lined the edges of the field in ragged lines, but these did not supply enough seats and many were standing. They weaved with a continual life; now and again the rider of one of the pitching horses bobbed above the crowd, and the rattle of voices sharpened, with piercing single calls. Always the dust of battle rose in shining wisps against the sun and Marianne approached with a sinking heart, for as she crossed the track and climbed through the fence she heard the snort and squeal of an angry, fear-tormented horse. The crying of a child could not have affected her so deeply.

The circle was too thick to be penetrated, it seemed, but as she drew closer an opening appeared and she easily sifted through to the front line of the circle. It was not the first time she had found that the way of women is made easy in the West. Just as she reached her place a horse scudded away from the far end of the field with a rider yelling; the swaying head and shoulders back. He seemed to be shrinking from such speed, but as a matter of fact he was poised and balanced nicely for any chance whirl. When it had gained full speed the broncho pitched high in the air, snapped its head and heels close together, and came down stiff-legged. Marianne sympathetically felt that impact jar home in her brain but the rider kept his seat. Worse was coming. For sixty seconds the horse was in an ecstasy of furious and educated bucking, flinging itself into odd positions and hitting the earth. Each whip-snap of that stinging struggling body jarred the rider shrewdly. Yet he clung in his place until the fight ended with startling suddenness. The grey dropped out of the air in a last effort and then stood head-down, quivering, beaten.

The victor jogged placidly back to the high-fenced corrals, with shouts of applause going up about him.

"Hey, lady," called a voice behind and above Marianne. "Might be you would like to sit up here with us?"

It was a high-bodied buckboard with two improvised seats behind the driver's place and Marianne thanked him with a smile. A fourteen-year-old stripling sprang down to help her but she managed the step-up without his hand. She was taken at once, and almost literally, into the bosom of the family, three boys, a withered father, a work-faded mother, all with curious, kindly eyes. They felt she was not their order, perhaps. The sun had darkened her skin but would never spoil it; into their sweating noonday she carried a morning-freshness, so they propped her in the angle of the driver's seat beside the mother and made her at home. Their name was Corson; their family had been in the West "pretty nigh onto always"; they had a place down the Taliaferro River; and they had heard about the Jordan ranch. All of this was huddled into the first two minutes. They brushed through the necessaries and got at the excitement of the moment.

"I guess they ain't any doubt," said Corson. "Arizona Charley wins. He won two years back, too. Minds me of Pete Langley, the way he rests in a saddle. Now where's this Perris gent? D'you see him? My, ain't they shouting for Arizona! Well, he's pretty bad busted up, but I guess he's still good enough to hold this Perris they talk about. Where's Perris?"

The same name was being shouted here and there in the crowd. Corson stood up and peered about him.

"Who is Perris?" asked Marianne.

"A gent that come out of the north, up Montana way, I hear. He's been betting on himself to win this bucking contest, covering everybody's money. A crazy man, he sure is!"

The voice drifted dimly to Marianne for she was falling into a pleasant haze, comfortably aware of eyes of admiration lifted to her more and more frequently from the crowd. She envied the blue coolness of the mountains, or breathed gingerly because the sting of alkali-dust was in the air, or noted with impersonal attention the flash of sun on a horse struggling in the far off corrals. The growing excitement of the crowd, as though a crisis were approaching, merely lulled her more. So the voice of Corson was half heard; the words were unconnotative sounds.

"Let the winner pick the worst outlaw in the lot. Then Perris will ride that hoss first. If he gets throwed he loses. If he sticks, then the other gent has just got to sit the same hoss—one that's already had the edge took off his bucking. Well, ain't that a fool bet?"

"It sounds fair enough," said Marianne. "Perris, I suppose, hasn't ridden yet. And Arizona Charley is tired from his work."

"Arizona tired? He ain't warmed up. Besides, he's got a hoss here that Perris will break his heart trying to ride. You know what hoss they got here today? They got Rickety! Yep, they sure enough got old Rickety!"

He pointed.

"There he comes out!"

Marianne looked lazily in the indicated direction and then sat up, wide awake. She had never seen such cunning savagery as was in the head of this horse, its ears going back and forth as it tested the strength of the restraining ropes. Now and then it crouched and shuddered under the detested burden of the saddle. It was a stout-legged piebald with the tell-tale Roman nose obviously designed for hard and enduring battle. He was a fighting horse as plainly as a terrier is a fighting dog.

Arizona Charley, a tall man off a horse and walking with a limp, moved slowly about the captive, grinning at his companions. It was plain that he did not expect the stranger to survive the test.

A brief, deep-throated shout from the crowd.

"There's Perris!" cried Corson. "There's Red Perris, I guess!"

Marianne gasped.

It was the devil-may-care cavalier who had laughed and fought and whistled under the window of her room. He stepped from the thick of the circle near Rickety and responded to the voice of the crowd by waving his hat. It would have been a trifle too grandiloquent had he not been laughing.

"He's going through with it," said Corson, shivering and chuckling at the same time. "He's going to try Rickety. They look like one and the same kind to me—two reckless devils, that hoss and Red Jim Perris!"

"Is there real danger?" asked Marianne.

Corson regarded her with pity.

"Rickety *can* be rode, they say," he answered, "but I disremember anybody that's done it. Look! He's a man-killer that hoss!"

Perris had stepped a little too close and the piebald thrust out at him with reaching teeth and striking forefoot. The man leaped back, still laughing.

"Cool, all right," said Corson judicially. "And maybe he ain't just a blow-hard, after all. There they go!"

It happened very quickly. Perris had shaken hands with Arizona, then turned and leaped into the saddle. The ropes were loosed. Rickety crouched a moment to feel out the reality of his freedom, then burst away with head close to the ground and ragged mane fluttering. There was no leaning back in this rider. He sat arrowy-straight save that his left shoulder worked back in convulsive jerks as he strove to get the head of Rickety up. But the piebald had the bit. Once his chin was tucked back against his breast his bucking chances were gone and he kept his nose as low as possible, like the trained fighter that he was. There were no yells now. They received Rickety as the appreciative receive a great artist—in silence.

The straight line of his flight broke into a crazy tangle of criss-cross pitching. Out of this maze he appeared again in a flash of straight galloping, used the impetus for a dozen jarring bucks, then reared and toppled backward to crush the cowpuncher against the earth.

Marianne covered her eyes, but an invisible power dragged her hand down and made her watch. She was in time to see Perris whisk out of the saddle before Rickety struck the dirt. His hat had been snapped from his head. The sun and the wind were in his flaming hair. Blue eyes and white teeth flashed as he laughed again.

"I like 'em mean," he had said, "and I keep 'em mean. A tame horse is like a tame man, and I don't give a damn for a fellow who won't fight!"

Once that had irritated her but now, remembering, it rang in her ear to a different tune. As Rickety spun to his feet, Perris vaulted to the saddle and found both stirrups in mid-leap, so to speak. The gelding instantly tested the firmness of his rider's seat by vaulting high and landing on one stiffened foreleg. The resultant shock broke two ways, like a curved ball, snapping down and jerking to one side. But he survived the blow, giving gracefully to it.

It was fine riding, very fine; and the crowd hummed with appreciation.

"A handsome rascal, eh?" said Mr. Corson.

But she caught at his arm.

"Oh!" gasped Marianne. "Oh! Oh!"

Three flurries of wild pitching drew forth those horrified whispers. But still the flaming red head of the rider was as erect, as jaunty as ever. Then the quirt flashed above him and cut Rickety's flank; the crowd winced and gasped. He was not only riding straight up but he was putting the quirt to Rickety—to Rickety!

The piebald seemed to feel the sting of the insult more than the lash. He bolted across the field to gain impetus for some new and more terrible feat but as he ran a yell from Perris thrilled across the crowd.

"They do that, some men. Get plumb drunk with a fight!"

But Marianne did not hear Corson's remark. She watched Rickety slacken his run as that longdrawn yell began, so wild and high that it put a tingle in her nose. Now he was trotting, now he was walking, now he stood perfectly still, become of a sudden, an abject, cowering figure. The shout of the spectators was almost a groan, for Rickety had been beaten fairly and squarely at last and it was like the passing of some old master of the prize ring, the scarred veteran of a hundred battles.

"What happened?" breathed Marianne.

"Rickety's lost his spirit," said Corson. "That's all. I've seen it come to the bravest men in the world. A two-year-old boy could ride Rickety now. Even the whip doesn't get a single buck out of the poor rascal."

The quirt slashed the flank of the piebald but it drew forth only a meek trot. The terrible Rickety went back to the corrals like a lamb!

"Arizona's got a good man to beat," admitted Corson, "but he's got a chance yet. They won't get any more out of Rickety. He's not only been rode— he's been broke. I could ride him myself."

"Mr. Corson," said Marianne, full of an idea of her own, "I'll wager that Rickety is not broken in the least—except for Red Perris."

"Meaning Perris just sort of put a charm on him?" suggested Corson, smiling.

"Exactly that. You see?"

In fact, the moment Perris slipped from the saddle, Rickety rocked forward on his forelegs and drove both heels at one of the reckless who came too near. A second later he was fighting with the activity and venom of a cat to get away from the ropes. The crowd chattered its surprise. Plainly the fierce old outlaw had not fought his last.

"What *did* Perris do to the horse?" murmured Marianne.

"I don't know," said Corson. "But you seem to have guessed something. See the way he stands there with his chin on his fist and studies Rickety! Maybe Perris is one of these here geniuses and us ordinary folks can only understand a genius by using a book on him."

She nodded, very serious.

"There *is* a use for fighting men, isn't there?" she brooded.

"Use for 'em?" laughed Corson. "Why, lady, how come we to be sitting here? Because gents have fought to put us here! How come this is part of God's country? Because a lot of folks buckled on guns to make it that! Use for a fighter? Well, Miss Jordan, I've done a little fighting of one kind and another in my day and I don't blush to think about it. Look at my kid there. What do you think I'm proudest of: because he was head of his class at school last winter or because he could lick every other boy his own size? First time he come home with a black eye I gave him a dollar to go back and try to give the other fellow *two* black eyes. And he done it! All good fighters ain't good men; I sure know that. But they never was a man that was good to begin with and was turned bad by fighting. They's a pile of bad men around these parts that fight like lions; but that part of 'em is good. Yes sirree, they's plenty of use for a fighting man! Don't you never doubt that!"

She smiled at this vehemence, but it reinforced a growing respect for Perris.

Then, rather absurdly, it irritated her to find that she was taking him so seriously. She remembered the ridiculous song:

"Oh, father, father William, I've seen your daughter dear.

Will you trade her for the brindled cow and the yellow steer?"

Marianne frowned.

The shout of the crowd called her away from herself. Far from broken by the last ride, the outlaw horse now seemed all the stronger for the exercise. Discarding fanciful tricks, he at once set about sun-fishing, that most terrible of all forms of bucking.

The name in itself is a description. Literally Rickety hurled himself at the sun and landed alternately on one stiffened foreleg and then the other. At each shock the chin of Arizona Charley was flung down against his chest and at the same time his head snapped sideways with the uneven lurch of the horse. An ordinary pony would have broken his leg at the first or second of these jumps; but Rickety was untiring. He jarred to the earth; he vaulted up again as from springs—over and over the same thing.

It would eventually have become tiresome to watch had not both horse and rider soon showed effects of the work. Every leap of Rickety's was shorter. Sweat shone on his thick body. He was killing Arizona but he was also breaking his own heart. Arizona weakened fast under that continual battering at the base of his brain. His eyes rolled. He no longer pretended to ride straight up, but clung to pommel and cantle. A trickle of blood ran from his mouth. Marianne turned away only to find that mild old Corson was crying: "Watch his head! When it begins to roll then you know that he's stunned and the next jump or so will knock him out of the saddle as limp as a half filled sack."

"It's too horrible!" breathed the girl. "I can't watch!"

"Why not? You liked it when a man beat a hoss. Now the tables are turned and the hoss is beating the man. Ah, I thought so. There goes his head! Rolls as if his neck was broken. Now! Now!"

Arizona Charley toppled loose-limbed from the saddle and lay twisted where he fell, but it had taken the last of Rickety's power. His legs were now braced, his head untriumphantly low, and the sweat dripped steadily from him. He had not enough energy to flee from those who approached to lift Arizona from the ground. Corson was pounding his knee with a fat fist.

"Ever see a fight like that in your life? Nope, you never did! Me neither! But Lord, Lord, won't Red Jim Perris take a mule-load of coin out of Glosterville! They been giving five to one agin him. I was touched a bit myself."

For the moment, Marianne was more keenly interested in the welfare of Arizona Charley. Perris, with others following, reached him first and strong hands carried the unconscious champion towards that corner of the field where the Corson buckboard stood; for there were the water-buckets. They were close to the goal when Arizona recovered sufficiently to kick himself loose feebly from his supporters.

"What the hell's all this?" Marianne heard him say in a voice which he tried to make an angered roar but which was only a shrill quaver from his weakness. "Maybe I'm a lady? Maybe I've fainted or something? Not by a damned sight! Maybe I been licked by that boiled-down bit of hell, Rickety, but I ain't licked so bad I can't walk home. Hey, Perris, shake on it! You trimmed me, all right, and you collect off'n me and a pile more besides me. Here's my boodle."

At the mention of the betting a little circle cleared around Perris and from every side hands full of greenbacks were thrust forward. The latter pushed back his sombrero and scratched his head, apparently deep in thought.

"It's a speech, boys," cried Arizona Charley, supporting himself on the shoulder of a friend. "Give Red air; give him room; he's going to make a speech!

And then we'll pay him for what he's got to say."

There was much laughter, much slapping of backs.

"That's Arizona," remarked Corson. "Ain't he a game loser?"

"He's a fine fellow," said the girl, with emotion. "My heart goes out to him!"

"Does it, now?" wondered Corson. "Well, I'd of figured more on Perris being the man for the ladies to look at. He's sure set up pretty! Now he makes his little talk."

"Ladies and gents," said Red Perris, turning the color of his sobriquet. "I ain't any electioneer when it comes to speech making."

"That's all right, boy," shouted encouraging partisans. "You'll get my vote if you don't say a word."

"But I'll make it short," said Perris. "It's about these bets. They're all off. It just come to my mind that two winters back me and this same Rickety had a run in up Montana-way and he come out second-best. Well, he must of remembered me the way I just now remembered him. That's why he plumb quit when I let out a whoop. If he'd turned loose all his tricks like he done with Arizona, why most like Charley would never of had to take his turn. I'd be where he is now and he'd be doing the laughing. Anyway, boys, the bets are off. I don't take money on a sure thing."

It brought a shout of protest which was immediately drowned in a hearty yell of applause.

"Now, don't that warm your heart, for you?" said Corson as the noise fell away a little. "I tell you what—" he broke off with a chuckle, seeing that she had taken a pencil and a piece of paper from her purse and was scribbling hastily: "Taking notes on the Wild West, Miss Jordan?"

"Mental notes," she said quietly, but smiling at him as she folded the slip. She turned to the stripling, who all this time had hardly taken his eyes from her even to watch the bucking and to hear the speech of Perris.

"Will you take this to Jim Perris for me?"

A gulp, a grin, a nod, he was down from the wagon in a flash and using his leanness to wriggle snakelike through the crowd.

"Well!" chuckled Corson, not unkindly, "I thought it would be more Perris than Arizona in the wind-up!"

She reddened, but not because of his words. She was thinking of the impulsive note in which she asked Red Perris to call at the hotel after the race and ask for Marianne Jordan. Remembering his song from the street, she wondered if he, also, would have the grace to blush when they met.

CHAPTER IV
THE STRENGTH OF THE WEAK

BY simply turning about the crowd was in position to watch the race. Of course it packed dense around the finish on both sides of the lane but Corson had chosen his position well, the white posts were not more than a dozen yards above them and they would be able to see the rush of horses across the line. It was pleasant to Marianne to turn her back on the scene of the horse-breaking and face her own world which she knew and loved.

The ponies were coming out to be paraded for admiration and to loosen their muscles with a few stretching gallops. Each was ridden by his owner, each bore a range saddle. To one accustomed to jockeys and racing-pads, these full-grown riders and cumbrous trappings made the cowponies seem small but they were finely formed, the pick of the range. The days of mongrel breeds are long since over in the West. Smaller heads, longer necks, more sloping shoulders, told of good blood crossed on the range stock. Still, the base-stock showed clearly when the Coles mares came onto the track with mincing steps, turning their proud heads from side to side and every one coming hard on the bit. Coles had taken no chances, and though he had been forced by the rules of the race to put up the regulation range saddles he had found the lightest riders possible. Their small figures brought out the legginess of the mares; beside the compact range horses their gait was sprawling, but the wise eye of Marianne saw the springing fetlocks kiss the dust and the long, telltale muscles. She cried out softly in admiration and pleasure.

"You see the Coles mares?" she said. "There go the winners, Mr. Corson. The ponies won't be in it after two furlongs."

Corson regarded her with a touch of irritation: "Now, don't you be too sure, lady," he growled. "Lots of legs, I grant you. Too much for me. Are they pure bred?"

"No," she answered, "there's enough cold blood to bring the price down. But Coles is a wise business man. After they've won this race in a bunch they'll look, every one, like daughters of Salvator. See that! Oh, the beauties!"

One of the range horses was loosed for a fifty yard sprint and as he shot by, the mares swayed out in pursuit. There was a marked difference between the gaits. The range horse pounded heavily, his head bobbing; the mares stepped out with long, rocking gallop. They seemed to be going with half the effort and less than half the speed, and yet, strangely, they very nearly kept up with the sprinter until their riders took them back to the eager, prancing walk. Marianne's eyes sparkled but the little exhibition told a different story to old Corson. He snorted with pleasure.

"Maybe you seen that, Miss Jordan? You seen Jud Hopkin's roan go by them fancy Coles mares? Well, well, it done my heart good! This gent Coles comes out of the East to teach us poor ignorant ranchers what right hoss flesh should be. He's going to auction off them half dozen mares after the race. Well, sir, I wouldn't give fifty dollars a head for 'em. Nor neither will nobody else when they see them mares fade away in the home stretch; nope, neither will nobody else."

In this reference to over-wise Easterners there was a direct thrust at the girl, but she accepted it with a smile.

"Don't you think they'll last for the mile and a quarter, Mr. Corson?"

"Think? I don't think. I know! Picture hosses like them—well, they'd ought to be left in books. They run a little. Inside a half mile they bust down. Look how long they are!"

"But their backs are short," put in Marianne hastily.

"Backs short?" scoffed Corson, "Why, lady look for yourself!"

She choked back her answer. If the self-satisfied old fellow could not see how far back the withers reached and how far forward the quarters, so that the true back was very short, it was the part of wisdom to let experience teach him. Yet she could not refrain from saying: "You'll see how they last in the race, Mr. Corson."

"We'll both see," he answered. "There goes a gent that's going to lose money today!"

A big red-faced man with his hat on the back of his head and sweat coursing down his cheeks, was pushing through the crowd calling with a great voice:

"Here's Lady Mary money. Evens or odds on Lady Mary!" "That's Colonel Dickinson," said Corson. "He comes around every year to play the races here and most generally he picks winners. But today he's gone wrong. His eye has been took by the legs of them Coles hosses and he's gone crazy betting on 'em. Well, he gets plenty of takers!"

Indeed, Colonel Dickinson was stopped right and left to record wagers.

"I got down a little bet myself, this morning, agin his Lady Mary." Corson chuckled at the thought of such easy money.

"What makes you so sure?" asked Marianne, for even if she were lucky enough to get the mares she felt that from Corson she could learn beforehand the criticisms of Lew Hervey.

"So sure? Why anybody with half an eye—" here he remembered that he was talking to a lady and continued more mildly. "Them bay mares ain't hosses—they're tricks. Look how skinny all that underpinning is, Miss Jordan."

"When they fill out—" she began.

"Tush! They won't never fill out proper. Too much leg to make a hoss. Too much daylight under 'em. Besides, what good would they be for cow-work? High headed fools, all of 'em, and a hoss that don't know enough to run with his head low can't turn on a forty acre lot. Don't tell me!"

He forbade contradiction by raising an imperious hand. Marianne was so exasperated that she looked to Mrs. Corson in the pinch, but that old lady was smiling dimly behind her glasses; she seemed to be studying the smoky gorges of the Eagles, so Marianne wisely deferred her answer and listened to that unique voice which rises from a crowd of men and women when horses are about to race. There is no fellow to the sound. The voice of the last-chance better is the deep and mournful burden; the steady rattle of comment is the body of it; and the edge of the noise is the calling of those who are confident with "inside dope." Marianne, listening, thought that the sound in Glosterville was very much like the sound in Belmont. The difference was in the volume alone. The hosses were now lining up for the start, it was with a touch of malice that Marianne said: "I suppose that's one of your range types? That faded old chestnut just walking up to get in line?"

Corson started to answer and then rubbed his eyes to look again.

It was Alcatraz plodding towards the line of starters, his languid hoofs rousing a wisp of dust at every step. He went with head depressed, his sullen; hopeless ears laid back. On his back sat Manuel Cordova, resplendent in sky-blue, tight-fitting jacket. Yet he rode the spiritless chestnut with both hands, his body canted forward a little, his whole attitude one of desperate alertness. There was something so ludicrous in the contrast between the hair-trigger nervousness of the Mexican and the drowsy unconcern of the stallion that a murmur of laughter rose from the crowd about the starting line and drifted across the field.

"I suppose you'll say that long hair is good to keep him warm in winter," went on the girl sarcastically. "As far as legs are concerned, he seems to have about as much as the longest of the mares."

Corson shook his head in depreciation.

"You never can tell what a fool Mexican will do. Most like he's riding in this race to show off his jacket, not because he has any hope of winning. That hoss ain't any type of range—"

"Perhaps you think it's a thoroughbred?" asked Marianne.

Corson sighed, feeling that he was cornered.

"Raised on the range, all right," he admitted. "But you'll find freak hosses anywhere. And that chestnut is just a plug."

"And yet," ventured Marianne, "it seems to me that the horse has some points."

This remark drew a glance of scorn from the whole Corson family. What would they think, she wondered, if they knew that her hopes centered on this very stallion? Silence had spread over the field. The whisper of Corson seemed loud. "Look how still the range hosses stand. They know what's ahead. And look at them fool bays prance!"

The Coles horses were dancing eagerly, twisting from side to side at the post.

"Oh!" cried Mrs. Corson. "What a vicious brute!"

Alcatraz had wakened suddenly and driven both heels at his neighbor. Luckily he missed his mark, but the starter ran across the track and lessoned Cordova with a raised finger. Then he went back; there was a breath of waiting; the gun barked!

The answer to it was a spurt of low-running horses with a white cloud of dust behind, and Corson laughed aloud in his glee. Every one of the group in the lead was a range horse; the Coles mares were hanging in the rear and last of all, obscured by the dust-cloud, Alcatraz ran sulkily.

"But you wait!" said Marianne, sitting tensely erect. "Those ponies with their short legs can start fast, but that's all. When the mares begin to run—Now, now, now! Oh, you beauties! You dears!"

The field doubled the first jagged corner of the track and the bay mares, running compactly grouped, began to gain on the leaders hand over hand. Looking first at the range hosses and then at the mares, it seemed that the former were running with twice the speed of the latter, but the long, rolling gallop of the bays ate up the ground, and bore them down on the leaders in a bright hurricane. The cowpunchers, hearing that volleying of hoofbeats, went to spur and quirt to stave off the inevitable, but at five furlongs Lady Mary left her sisters and streaked around the tiring range horses into the lead. Marianne cried out in delight. She had forgotten her hope that the mares might not win. All she desired now was that blood might tell and her judgment be vindicated.

"They won't last," Corson was growling, his voice feeble in the roar of the excited crowd. "They can't last that pace. They'll come back after a while and the ponies will walk away to the finish."

"Have you noticed," broke in Mrs. Corson, "that the poor old faded chestnut seems to be keeping up fairly well?"

For as the bay mares cut around into the lead, Alcatraz was seen at the heels of the range horses, running easily. It seemed, with a great elastic stride.

"But—but—it's not the same horse!" Marianne gasped.

To be sure, Alcatraz in motion was transformed, the hollows among his ribs forgotten, and the broken spirit replaced by power, the electric power of the racer.

"It looks very much to me as if the Mexican is pulling that horse, too," said Marianne. For Cordova rode with legs braced, keeping a tight pull that bent the head of Alcatraz down. He might have served for a statue of fear. "And notice that he makes no effort to break around the range horses or through them. What's the matter with him?"

At seven furlongs the mares were in a group of themselves, lengths in front and drawing away; the heads of the cowponies were going up, sure sign that they were spent, and even Corson was gloomily silent. He was remembering his bet against Lady Mary, and lo, Lady Mary was breezing in front well within her strength. One glance at her pricking ears told an eloquent story. Near them Marianne saw big Colonel Dickinson capering. And the sight inspired a shrewd suspicion. What if he knew the reputation of Alcatraz and to secure his bets on Lady Mary, had bribed Cordova at the last moment to pull his horse. Certainly it seemed that was what the Mexican was doing.

"There's a lady," the colonel was shouting. "Go it, girl. Go it, beauty. Lady Mary! Lady Mary!"

Marianne raised her field glasses and studied the rush of horses through the fog of dust.

"It's just as I thought," she cried, without lowering the glasses. "The scoundrel is pulling Alcatraz! He rides as if he were afraid of something—afraid that the horse might break away. Look, Mr. Corson."

"I dunno," said Corson. "It sure does look sort of queer!"

"Why, he's purposely keeping that horse in a pocket. Has him on the rail. Oh, the villain!" It was a cry of shrill rage. "*He's sawing on the bit!* And the chestnut has his ears back. I can see the glint of his eyes. As if he wants to run simply because he is being held. But there— there—there! He's got the bit in his teeth. His head goes out. Mr. Corson, is it too late for Alcatraz to win the race?"

She dropped the glasses. There was no need of them now. Rounding into the long home stretch Cordova made a last frightened effort to regain control and then gave up, his eyes rolling with fear; Alcatraz had got his head.

He ran his own race from that point. He leaped away from the cowponies in the first three strides and set sail for the leaders. Because of his ragged appearance his name had been picked up by the crowd and sent drifting about the field; now they called on him loudly. For every rancher and every ranchhand in Glosterville was summoning Alcatraz to vindicate the range-stock against the long-legged mares which had been imported from the East for the sole purpose of shaming the native products. The cry shook in a wailing chorus across the field: "Alcatraz!" and again: "Alcatraz!" With tingling cowboy yells in between. And mightily the chestnut answered those calls, bolting down the stretch.

The riders of the mares had sensed danger in the shouting of the crowd, and though their lead seemed safe they took no chances but sat down and began to ride out their mounts. Still Alcatraz gained. From the stretching head, across the withers, the straight-driving croup, the tail whipped out behind, was one even line. His ears were not flagging back like the ears of a horse merely giving his utmost of speed; they were dressed flat by a consuming fury, and the same uncanny rage gleamed in his eyes and trembled in his expanding nostrils. It was like a human effort and for that reason terrible in a brute beast. Marianne saw Colonel Dickinson with the fingers of one hand buried in his plump breast; the other had reared his hat aloft, frozen in place in the midst of the last flourish; and never in her life had she seen such mingled incredulity and terror.

She looked back again. There were three sections to the race now. The range ponies were hopelessly out of it. The Coles horses ran well in the lead. Between, coming with tremendous bounds, was Alcatraz. He got no help from his rider. The light jockey on Lady Mary was aiding his mount by throwing his weight with the swing of her gallop, but Manuel Cordova was a leaden burden. The most casual glance showed the man to be in a blue funk; he rode as one astride a thunderbolt and Alcatraz had both to plan his race and run it.

A furlong from the finish he caught the rearmost of the mares and cut around them, the dust spurting sidewise. The crowd gasped, for as he passed the bays it was impossible to judge his speed accurately; and after the breath of astonishment the cheers broke in a wave. There was a confusion of emotion in Marianne. A victory for the chestnut would be a coup for her pocketbook when it came to buying the Coles horses, but it would be a distinct blow to her pride as a horsewoman. Moreover, there was that in the stallion which roused instinctive aversion. Hatred for Cordova sustained him, for there was no muscle in the lean shoulders or the starved quarters to drive him on at this terrific pace.

In the corner of her vision she saw old Corson, agape, pale with excitement, swiftly beating out the rhythm of Alcatraz's swinging legs; and then she looked to Lady Mary. Every stride carried the bay back to the relentless stallion. Her head had not yet gone up; she was still stretched out in the true racing form; but there was a roll in her gallop. Plainly Lady Mary was a very, very tired horse.

She shot in to the final furlong with whip and spur lifting her on, every stroke brought a quivering response; all that was in her strong heart was going into this race. And still the chestnut gained. At the sixteenth her flying tail was reached by his nose And still he ate up the distance. Yet spent as the mare was, the chestnut was much farther gone. If there was a roll in her weary gallop, there was a stagger in his gait; still he was literally flinging himself towards the finish. No help from his rider certainly, but every rancher in the crowd was shouting hoarsely and swinging himself towards the finish as though that effort of will and body might, mysteriously, be transmitted to the struggling horse and give him new strength.

Fifty yards from the end his nose was at Lady Mary's shoulder and Marianne saw the head of the mare jerk up. She was through but the stallion was through also. He had staggered in his stride, drunkenly. She saw him shake his head, saw him fling forward again, and the snaky head crept once more to the neck of the mare, to her ears, and on and on.

Five hundred voices bellowed his name to lift him to the finish: "Alcatraz!" Then they were over the line and the riders were pulling up. It was not hard to stop Alcatraz. He went by Marianne at a reeling trot, his legs shambling weakly and his head drooping, a weary rag of horseflesh with his ears still gloomily flattened to his neck.

But who had won? The uproar was so terrific that Marianne could not distinguish the name of the victor as the judges called it, waving their arms to command silence. Then she saw Colonel Dickinson walking with fallen head. The fat man was sagging in his step. His face had grown pale and pouchy in the moment. And she knew that the ragged chestnut had indeed conquered. Courage is the strength of the weak but in Alcatraz hatred had occupied that place.

CHAPTER V
RETRIBUTION

COLES had advertised the auction sale of the mares to take place immediately after the race and though he would gladly have postponed it he had to live up to his advertisement. Naturally the result was disastrous. The ranchers had seen the ragged Alcatraz win against the imported horses and they felt they could only show their local patriotism by failing to bid. There were one or two mocking offers of a hundred dollars a head for the lot. "Something pretty for my girl to ride," as one of the ranchers phrased it, laughing. The result was that every one of the mares was knocked down to Marianne at a ludicrously low price; so low that when it was over and Coles strolled about with her to indicate the size of her bargain she felt that she was moving in a dream.

"It's easy to see that you're not Western," he said in the end, "but you have a Western horse to thank for putting this deal through—I mean Alcatraz."

"He's too ugly for that," said Marianne, and yet on her way back to the hotel she realized that the sun-faded chestnut had truly proved a gold mine to her. It had been, she felt, the luckiest day of her business life, for she knew that the price she had paid for the mares was less than half a reasonable valuation of them. Here was her ranch ready stocked, so to speak, with fine horses. It only needed, now, to end the tyrannical sway of Lew Hervey and in that fighting man of men, Red Perris, Marianne felt that the solution lay.

Once in her room at the hotel, she looked about her in some dismay. Of course she was merely an employer receiving a prospective employee to examine his qualifications, but she also remained, in spite of herself, a girl receiving a man. She was glad that no one was there to watch with quizzical eye as she rearranged the furniture; she was doubly glad that he could not watch her at the mirror. She gave herself the most critical examination since she left the East and on the whole she approved of the changes. The stirring life in the open had darkened the olive of her skin, she found, but also had made it more translucent; the curve of her cheek was pleasantly filled; her throat rounder; her head better poised. And above all excitement gave her the vital color.

She paused at this point to wonder why a stray cowpuncher should make her flush but immediately decided that he had nothing to do with it; it was the purchase of the mares that kept alive the little thrill of happiness. But Marianne was essentially honest and when her heart jumped as she heard a swift, light step come down the hall and pause at her door, she admitted at once that horses had nothing to do with the matter.

She wished ardently that she had made the discovery sooner. As it was, before she composed herself, he had knocked, been bidden in and stood before her. She knew, inwardly dismayed, that her eyes were wide, her color high, and her whole expression one of childish expectancy. It comforted her greatly to find that he was hardly more at ease than she. He made futile efforts to rub some dust from his shirt.

"I wanted to get fixed up," he said, "but the note said to come *right* after the race—Miss Jordan."

In fact he made a harum-scarum figure. The fight with him of the moustaches had produced rents invisible at a distance but distinct at close hand and the dust and the sweat had faded the blue of his shirt and the red of his bandana. But the red flame of that hair and the keen blue of that eye—they, to be sure, were not faded. She discovered other things as he crossed the room to her. That he was far shorter than he had seemed when he fought in the street. Indeed, he was middle height and slenderly made at that. She felt that looking at him from her window and watching him ride Rickety she had only seen the spirit of the man and not the physical fact at all.

He shook hands. She was glad to see that he neither peered at her slyly as a vain man is apt to do when he meets a girl who has sought him out nor met her sullenly as is the habit of the bashful Westerner. His head was high, his glance straight, and his smile appreciated her with frank enjoyment.

She tried to match her speech with his outright demeanor: "I have a business offer to make. I won't take a great deal of your time. Ten minutes will do. Won't you sit down, Mr. Perris?"

She took his tattered hat and pointed out a seat to him, noting, as she herself sat down, that he was as erect in his chair as he had been standing. There was something so adventurously restless about Red Perris that she thought of a thoroughbred fresh from the stable; just as a blooded hunter is apt to be "too much horse under the saddle," so she was inclined to feel that Perris was "too much man." Something about him was always moving. Either his lean fingers fretted on the arm of the chair, or his foot stirred, or his glance flickered, or his head turned proudly. Going back to the thoroughbred comparison she decided that Perris badly needed to have a race or two under his belt before he would be worked down to normal. She noted another thing: at close hand he was more handsome.

In the meantime, since she had to talk, it would be pleasanter to find some indirect approach. One was offered by the fob which hung outside the watchpocket of his trousers. It was a tarnished, misshapen lump of metal.

"I can't help asking about that fob," she said. "I've never seen one even remotely like it."

He fingered it with a singular smile.

"Tell you about it," he said amiably enough. "I was standing by looking at a large-sized fracas one day and me doing nothing—just as peaceful as an old plough-hoss—when a gent ups and drills me in the leg. His bullet had to cut through my holster and then it jammed into my thigh bone. Put me in bed for a couple of months and when I got out I had the slug fixed up for a fob. Just so's I could remember the man that shot me. That's about five years back. I ain't found him yet, but I'm still remembering, you see?"

He finished the anecdote with a chuckle which died out as he saw her eyes widen with horror. Five years ago? she was thinking, he must have been hardly more than a boy. How many other chapters as violent as this were in his story?

"And—he didn't even offer to pay your doctor bill, I'll wager?"

"Him?" Perris chuckled again. "He'll pay it, some day. It's just postponed— slow collection—that's all!" He shrugged the thought of it away, and straightened a little, plainly waiting to hear her business. But her mind was still only half on her own affairs as she began talking.

"I have to go into the affairs of our ranch a little," she said, "so that you can understand why I've asked you to come here. My father was hurt by a fall from a horse several years ago and the accident made him an invalid. He can't sit a saddle and because of that he has lost all touch with his business. Worst of all, he doesn't seem to care. The result was that everything went into the hands of the foreman, but the foreman was not very successful. As a matter of fact the ranch became a losing investment and I came out to try to run it. I suppose that sounds foolish?"

She looked sharply at him, but to her delight for the first time his eyes had lighted with a real enthusiasm.

"It sounds pretty fine to me," said Red Perris.

"The foreman doesn't think so," she answered. "He wants his old authority."

"So he makes your trail all uphill?"

"By simply refusing to advise me. My father won't talk business. Lew Hervey won't. I'm trying to run a dollar business with a cent's worth of knowledge and no experience. I can't discharge Hervey; his service has been too long and faithful. But I want to have someone up there who will go into training to take Hervey's place eventually. Someone who knows cattle and can tell me what to do now and then. Mr. Perris, do you know the cow business?"

Some of his interest faded.

"Most folks raised in these parts do," he answered obliquely. "I should think you could get a dozen anywhere."

She explained eagerly: "It's not so simple. You see, Lew Hervey is rather a rough character. In the old days I think he was quite a fighter. I guess he still is. And he's gathered a lot of fighting men for cowpunchers on the ranch. When he sees me bring in an understudy for his part, so to speak, I'm afraid he might make trouble unless he was convinced it would be safer to keep his hands off the new man."

The gloom of Perris returned. He was still politely attentive, but his head turned, and the eager eyes found something of interest across the street. She knew her grip on him was failing and she struggled to regain it. Here was her man, she knew. Here was one who would ride the fiercest outlaw horse on the ranch; wear out the toughest cowboy; play with them to weariness when they wanted to play, fight with them to exhaustion when they wanted to fight, and as her right-hand man, advise her for the best.

"As for terms, the right man can make them for himself," she concluded, hopelessly: "Mr. Perris, I think you could be the man for the place. What do you say to trying?"

He paused, diffidently, and she knew that in the pause he was hunting for polite terms of refusal.

"I'll tell you how it is. You're mighty kind to make the offer. You haven't seen much of me and that little bit has been—pretty rough." He laughed away his embarrassment. "So I appreciate your confidence—a lot. But I'm afraid that I'd be a tolerable lot like Hervey." He hurried on lest she should take offense. "You see, I don't like orders."

"Of course if it were a man who made the offer to you—" she began angrily.

He raised his hand. There were little touches of formal courtesy in him so contrasted with what she had seen of him in action, so at variance with the childishly gaudy clothes he wore, that it put Marianne completely at sea.

"It's just that I like my own way. I've been a rolling stone all my life. About the only moss I've gathered is what you see." He touched the dust-tarnished gold braid on his sombrero and his twinkling eyes invited her to mirth. But Marianne was sternly silent. She knew that her color was gone and that her beauty had in large part gone with it; a reflection that did not at all help her mood or her looks. "I get my fun out of playing a free hand," he was concluding. "I don't like partners. Not that I'm proud of it, but so you can see where I stand. If I don't like a bunkie you can figure why I don't want a boss."

She nodded stiffly, and at the unamiable gesture she saw him shrug his shoulders very slightly, his eyes wandered again as though he were seeking for a means to end the interview.

Marianne rose.

"I see your viewpoint, Mr. Perris," she said coldly. "And I'm sorry you can't accept my offer."

He came to his feet at the same moment, but still he lingered a moment, turning his hat thoughtfully so that she hoped, for an instant, that he was on the verge of reconsidering. After all, she should have used more persuasion; she was firmly convinced that at heart men are very close to children. Then his head went up and he shook away the mood which had come over him.

"Some time I'll come to it," he admitted. "But not yet a while. I take it mighty kind of you to have thought I could fill the bill and—I'm wishing you all sorts of luck, Miss Jordan."

"Thank you," said Marianne, and hated herself for her unbending stiffness.

At the door he turned again.

"I sure hope it's easy for you to forget songs," he said.

"Songs?" echoed Marianne, and then turned crimson with the memory.

"'You see," explained Red Jim Perris, "it's a bad habit I've picked up— of doing the first fool thing that comes into my head. Good-bye, Miss Jordan."

He was gone.

She felt, confusedly, that there were many thing? she should have said and at the same time there was a strange surety that sometime she would see him again and say them. She walked absently to the window which opened on the vacant lot to the rear of the hotel.

Red Perris vanished from her mind, for below her she saw Cordova in the act of tethering Alcatraz to the rack which stood in the middle of the lot; saddle and bridle had been removed—the stallion wore only a stout halter.

The Mexican kept on the far side of the rack and whipped his knot together hastily; it was not till he sprang back from his work that she saw the snaky length of an eight foot blacksnake uncoil from his hand. He passed the lash slowly through his fingers, while surveying the stallion with great complacence. The ears of Alcatraz flattened back, a sufficient proof that he knew what was coming; he maintained his weary attitude, but it now seemed one of despair. As for Marianne she refused to admit the ugly suspicion which began to occur to her. But Cordova left her only a moment for doubt.

The black streak curled around his head, and through the open window she heard the crack of the lash-end. Alcatraz did not stir under the blow. Once more the blacksnake whirled, and Cordova leaned back to give the stroke the full stretch of arm and body; yet Alcatraz did not so much as lift an ear. Only when the lash hung in mid-air did he stir. The rope which tethered him hung slack, and this enabled the stallion to give impetus to his backward leap. All the weight of his body, all the strain of his leg muscles snapped the rope taut. It vibrated to invisibility for an instant, then parted with a sound as loud as the fall of the whip. The straining body of Alcatraz, so released, toppled sidewise. He rolled like a dog in the dust, and when, with the agility of a dog, he gained his feet, Cordova was fleeing towards the hotel with a horror-stricken face.

Even then she could not understand his terror—not until she saw that Alcatraz had wheeled and was bolting in hot pursuit. He came like the "devil-horse" that the Mexican called him, with his ears flattened and his mouth gaping; he came with such velocity that Cordova, running as only consummate terror can make a man run, seemed to be racing on a treadmill—literally standing still.

The picket fence which set off the back yard of the hotel gave the man an instant of delay—a terribly vital instant, indeed, that seemed to Marianne to contain long, long minutes. But here he was over and running again. In her dread she wondered why he was not shrieking for aid, but the face of Cordova was rigid—a nightmare mask!

Twenty steps, now, to the hotel, and surely there was still hope. No, for Alcatraz sailed across the pickets with a bound that cut in two the distance still dividing him from his master. It had all happened, perhaps, within the space of three breaths. Now Marianne leaned out of the window and screamed her warning, for the faded chestnut was on the very heels of the Mexican. He raised his contorted face at her cry, then threw up both his arms to her in a gesture she could never forget.

"Shoot!" yelled Cordova. "Amigo, amigo, shoot! Quick—"

Then Alcatraz struck him!

Half the bones in his body must have been broken by the impact. It spun him over and over in the dust, yet as the impetus of the chestnut carried him far past, Cordova struggled to his feet and attempted to flee again. Alas, it was only a step! His left leg crumpled under him. He toppled sideways, still wriggling and twisting onwards through the dirt—and then Alcatraz struck him again.

This time is was no blind rush. Back and forth, up and down, he crossed and recrossed, wheeled and reared and stamped, until his one white stocking was crimsoned and spurts of red flew out and turned black in the dust.

The horror which had choked her relaxed and Marianne shrieked again. It was that second cry which saved a faint spark of life for Cordova for at the sound the stallion leaped sidewise from the body of his victim, lifted his head towards the half fainting girl in the window, and trumpeted a great neigh of defiance. Still neighing he swerved away into a gallop, cleared the fence a second time, and fled from view.

CHAPTER VI
FREEDOM

TOWARDS the Eagles, rolling up like wind-blown smoke, Alcatraz fled, cleared one by one the fences about the small fields near Glosterville, and so came at last to the broader domains under the foothills. Here, on a rise of ground, he halted for the first time and looked back.

The heat waves, glimmering up endlessly, obscured Glosterville, but the wind, from some hidden house among the hills, bore to him wood-smoke scents with a mingling of the abhorrent odors of man. It made many an old scar of spur-gore and biting whiplash tingle; it was a background of pain which was like seasoning for the new delight of freedom.

As though there was a poundage of joy and additional muscle in self-mastery, the frame of the chestnut filled, his neck arched, and there came into his eyes that gleam which no man can describe and which for lack of words he calls the light of the wild.

Fear, to be sure, was still with him; would ever be with him, for the thought of man followed like galloping horses surrounding him, but what a small shadow was that in the sunshine of this new existence! His life had been the bitterness of captivity since Cordova took in part payment of a drunken gambling debt a sickly foal out of an old thoroughbred mare. The sire was unknown, and Cordova, disgusted at having to accept this wretched horseflesh in place of money, had beaten the six months' old colt soundly and turned it loose in the pasture. There followed a brief season of happiness in the open pasture but when the new grass came, short and thick and sweet and crisp under tooth, Cordova came by the pasture and saw his yearling flirting away from the fastest of the older horses with a stretch gallop that amazed the Mexican. He leaned a moment on the fence watching with glittering eyes and then he passed into a dream. At the end of the dream he took Alcatraz out of the pasture and into the stable. That had been to Alcatraz, like the first calamity falling on Job, the beginning of sorrow and for three years and more he had endured not in patience but with an abiding hatred. For a great hatred is a great strength, and the hatred for Cordova made the chestnut big of heart to wait. He had learned to season his days with the patience of the lynx waiting for the porcupine to uncurl or the patience of the cat amazingly still for hours by the rat-hole. In such a manner Alcatraz endured. Once a month, or once a year, he found an opening to let drive at the master with his heels, or to rear and strike, or to snap with his teeth wolfishly. If he missed it meant a beating; if he landed it meant a beating postponed; and so the dream had grown to have the man one day beneath his feet. Now, on the hilltop, every nerve in his forelegs quivered in memory of the feel of live flesh beneath his stamping hoofs.

It is said that sometimes one victory in the driving finish of a close race will give a horse a great heart for running and one defeat, similarly, may break him. But Alcatraz, who had endured so many defeats, was at last victorious and the triumph was doubly sweet. It was not the work of chance. More than once he had tested the strength of that old halter rope, covertly, with none to watch, and had felt it stretch and give a little under the strain of his weight; but he had long since learned the futility of breaking ropes so long as there were stable walls or lofty corral fences to contain him. A moment of local freedom meant nothing, and he had waited until he should find open sky and clear country; this was his reward of patience.

The short, frayed end of the rope dangled beneath his chin; his neck stung where the rope had galled him; but these were minor ills and freedom was a panacea. Later he would work off the halter as he alone knew how. The wind, swinging sharply to the north and the west, brought the fragrance of the forests on the slopes of the Eagles, and Alcatraz started on towards them. He would gladly have waited and rested where he was but he knew that men do not give up easily. What one fails to do a herd comes to perform. Moreover, men struck by surprise, men stalked with infinite cunning; the moment when he felt most secure in his stall and ate with his head down, blinded by the manger, was the very moment which the Mexican had often chosen to play some cruel prank. The lip of Alcatraz twitched back from his teeth as he remembered. This lesson was written into his mind with the letters of pain: in the moment of greatest peace, beware of man!

That day he journeyed towards the mountains; that night he chose the tallest hill he could find and rested there, trusting to the wide prospect to give him warning; and no matter how soundly he slept the horrid odor of man approaching would bring him to his feet. No man came near but there were other smells in the night. Once the air near the ground was rank with fox. He knew that smell, but he did not know the fainter scent of wildcat. Neither could he tell that the dainty-footed killer had slipped up within half a dozen yards of his back and crouched a long moment yearning towards the mountain of warm meat but knowing that it was beyond its powers to make the kill.

A thousand futile alarms disturbed Alcatraz, for freedom gave the nights new meanings for him. Sometimes he wakened with a start and felt that the stars were the lighted lanterns of a million men searching for him; and sometimes he lay with his head strained high listening to the strange silence of the mountains and the night which has a pulse in it and something whispering, whispering forever in the distance. Hunted men have heard it and to Alcatraz it was equally filled with charm and terror. What made it he could not tell. Neither can men understand. Perhaps it is the calling of the wild animals just beyond ear shot. That overtone of the mountains troubled and frightened Alcatraz on his first night; eventually he was to come to love it.

He was up in the first grey of the dawn hunting for food and he found it in the form of bunchgrass. He had been so entirely a stable-raised horse that this fodder was new to him. His nose assured him over and over again that this was nourishment, but his eyes scorned the dusty patches eight or ten inches across and half of that in height, with a few taller spears headed out for seed. When he tried it he found it delicious, and as a matter of fact it is probably the finest grass in the world.

He ate slowly, for he punctuated his cropping of the grass with glances towards the mountains. The Eagles were growing out of the night, turning from purple-grey to purple-blue, to daintiest lavender mist in the hollows and rosy light on the peaks, and last the full morning came over the sky at a step and the day wind rose and fluffed his mane.

He regarded these changes with a kindly eye, much as one who has never seen a sunrise before; and just as he had always made the corral into which he was put his private possession, and dangerous ground for any other creature, so now he took in the down-sweep of the upper range and the big knees of the mountains pushing out above the foothills and the hills themselves modelled softly down towards the plain, and it seemed to Alcatraz that this was one great corral, his private property. The horizon was his fence, advancing and receding to attend him; all between was his proper range. He took his station on a taller hilltop and gave voice to his lordliness in a neigh that rang and re-rang down a hollow. Then he canted his head and listened. A bull bellowed an answer fainter than the whistle of a bird from the distance, and just on the verge of earshot trembled another sound. Alcatraz did not know it, but it made him shudder; before long he was to recognize the call of the lofer wolf, that grey ghost which runs murdering through the mountains.

Small though the sounds were, they convinced Alcatraz that his claim to dominion would be mightily disputed. But what is worth having at all if it is not worth fighting for? He journeyed down the hillside stepping from grass knot to grass knot. All the time he kept his sensitive nostrils alert for the ground-smell of water and raised his head from moment to moment to catch the upper-air scents in case there might be danger. At length, before prime, he came down-wind from a water-hole and galloped gladly to it. It was a muddy place with a slope of greenish sun-baked earth on all sides. Alcatraz stood on the verge, snuffed the stale odor in disgust and then flirted the surface water with his upper lip before he could make himself drink. Yet the taste was far from evil, and there was nothing of man about it. Yonder a deer had stepped, his tiny footprint sun-burned into the mud, and there was the sprawling, sliding track of a steer.

Alcatraz stepped further in. The feel of the cool slush was pleasant, working above his hoofs and over the sensitive skin of the fetlock joint. He drank again, bravely and deep, burying his nose as a good horse should and gulping the water. And when he came out and stamped the mud from his feet he was transformed. He had slept and eaten and drunk in his own home.

After that, he idled through the hills eating much, drinking often, and making up as busily as he could in a few weeks for the long years of semi-starvation under the regime of the Mexican. His body responded amazingly. His coat grew sleek, his barrel rounded, his neck arched with new muscles and the very quality of mane and tail changed; he became the horse of which he had previously been the caricature. It was a lonely life in many ways but the very loneliness was sweet to the stallion. Moreover, there was much to learn, and his brain, man-trained by his long battle against a man, drank in the lessons of the wild country with astonishing rapidity. Had it not been for intervention from the

Great Enemy, he might have continued for an indefinite period in the pleasant foothills.

But Man found him. It was after some weeks, while he was intently watching a chipmunk colony one day. Each little animal chattered at the door of his home and so intent was Alcatraz's attention that he had no warning of the approach of a rider up the wind until the gravel close behind spurted under the rushing hoofs of another horse and the deadly shadow of the rope swept over him. Terror froze him for what seemed a long moment under the swing of the rope, in reality his side-leap was swift as the bound of the wild cat and the curse of the unlucky cowpuncher roared in his ear.

Alcatraz shot away like a thrown stone. The pursuit lasted only five minutes, but to the stallion it seemed five ages, with the shouting of the man behind him, for while he fled every scar pricked him and once again his bones ached from every blow which the Mexican had struck. At the end of the five minutes Alcatraz was hopelessly beyond reach and the cowpuncher merely galloped to the highest hilltop to watch the runner. As far as he could follow the course, that blinding speed was not abated, and the cowpuncher watched with a lump growing in his throat. He had fallen into a dream of being mounted on a stallion which no horse in the mountains could overtake and which no horse in the mountains could escape. To be safe in flight, to be inescapable in pursuit—that was, in a small way, to be like a god.

But when Alcatraz disappeared in the horizon haze, the cowpuncher lowered his head with a sigh. He realized that such a creature was not for him, and he turned his horse's head and plodded back towards the ranchhouse. When he arrived, he told the first story of the wild red-chestnut, beautiful, swift as an eagle. He talked with the hunger and the fire which comes on the faces of those who love horses. It was not his voice but his manner which convinced his hearers, and before he ended every eye in the bunkhouse was lighted.

That moment was the beginning of the end for Alcatraz. From the moment men saw him and desired him the days of his freedom were limited; but great should be the battle before he was subdued!

CHAPTER VII
THE PROMISED LAND

THERE was no thought of submission in Alcatraz at this moment, though never for an instant did he under-rate the power of man. To Alcatraz the Mexican was the type, and Cordova had seemed to unite in himself many powers—strength like a herd of bulls, endurance greater than the contemptible patience of the burro, speed like the lightning which winks in the sky one instant and shatters the cottonwood tree the next. Such as he were men, creatures who conquer for the sake of conquest and who torment for the love of pain. His fear equalled his hatred, and his hatred made him shake with fever.

The horseman had vanished but it was not well to trust to mere distance. Had he not heard, more than once, the gun speaking from the hand of Cordova, and presently the wounded hawk fluttered out of the sky and dropped at the feet of the man? So Alcatraz kept on running. Besides, he rejoiced in the gallop. He was like a boy who leaves his strength untested for several years and when the crisis comes finds himself a man. So the red-chestnut marvelled at the new wells of strength which he was draining as he ran. That power which the Mexican had kept at low tide with his systematic brutality was now developed to the full, very near; and to Alcatraz it seemed exhaustless. He did not stop to look about until two miles of climbing up the steep sides of the Eagles had winded him.

He had risen above the foothills and the more laborious slopes of the Eagles lifted at angles sheer and more sheer towards the top. But decidedly he must cross the mountains. On the other side perhaps, there would be no men. There could be no better time. Already the hollow gorges were beginning to brim with blue-grey shadows and he would be taking the worst of the climb in the cool of the evening. So Alcatraz gave himself to the climb.

It was bitter work. Had he dropped a few miles south across the foothills he would have found the road to the Jordan ranch climbing up the Eagles with leisurely swinging curves, but the slopes just above him were heart-breaking, and Alcatraz began to realize in an hour that a mountainside from a distance is a far gentler thing than the same slope underfoot. It was the heart of twilight before he came to the middle of his climb and stepped onto a nearly level shoulder some acres in compass. Here he stood for a moment while the muscles, cramped from climbing, loosened again, and he looked down at the work he had already accomplished. It was a dizzy fall to the lowlands. The big foothills were mere dimples on the earth and limitless plain moved east towards darkness. The stallion breathed deep of the pure mountain air, contented. All his old life lay low beneath him in a thicker air and in a deeper night. He had climbed out of it to a lonely height, perhaps, but a free one. The wind, coming off the mountain top, curled his tail along his flank. He turned and put his head into it, already refreshed for more climbing. There was a strange scent in that wind, a rank, keen odor that would have stopped him instantly had he been wiser in the life of the wilderness. As it was, he trotted on through a skirting of shrubbery and on the verge of a clearing was stopped by a snarl that rolled out of the ground at his feet. Then he saw a dead deer on the ground and over it a great tawny creature. One paw lay on the flank of its prey; the bloody muzzle was just above.

There is no greater coward than the puma. Ordinarily she would have hesitated before attacking the grown horse, but the surprise made her desperate. She sprang even as Alcatraz whirled for flight, and in whirling he saw that there was no escape from the leap of this monster with the yawning teeth. He kicked high and hard, eleven hundred pounds of seasoned muscle concentrated in the drive. The blow would have smashed in the side of a bull. One hoof glanced off, but the other struck fair and full between the eyes of the mountain-lion. The great cat spun backwards, screeching, but Alcatraz saw no more than the fall. He fled up the mountain with fear of death lightening his strides, regardless of footing, crashing through underbrush, and came to the end of his hysterical flight at the crest of the slope.

There he paused, shaking and weak, but the mountain top was bare of covert, and scanning it eagerly through the treacherous moonlight he saw there was no immediate danger. Down the Western slopes he saw a fairyland for horses. Far beyond rose a second range nearly as lofty as the peak on which he stood, but in between tumbled rolling ground, a dreamy panorama in the moonshine. One feature was clear, and that was a broad looping of silver among the hills, a river with slender tributaries dodging swiftly down to it from either side. Alcatraz looked with a swelling heart, thinking of the white-hot deserts which he had known all his life. The wind which lifted his mane and cooled his hot body carried up, also, the delicious fragrance of the evergreens and it seemed to Alcatraz that he had come in view of a promised land. Surely he had dreamed of it on many a day in burning, dusty corrals or in oven-like sheds.

The descent was far less precipitous than the climb and far shorter to the plateau. Just where the true mountains broke out into a pleasant medley of foothills, the stallion stopped to rest. He nibbled a few mouthfuls of grass growing lush and rank on the edge of a watercourse, waded to the knees in a still pool and blotted out the star-images with the disturbance of his drinking, and then went back onto a hilltop to sleep.

It was full day before he rose and started on again, and to keep his strength for the next stage of the journey, he ate busily first on the lee side of a hill where the grass was thickest and tenderest. Between mouthfuls he raised his head to gaze down on his new-found land. It was a day of clouds, thin sheetings and dense cumulus masses sweeping on the west wind and breaking against the mountains. Alcatraz could not see the crests over which he had climbed the night before, so thick were those breaking ranks of clouds, but the plateau beneath him was dotted with yellow sunshine and in the day it filled to the full the promise of the moonlit night. He saw wide stretches of meadow; he saw hills sharpsided and smoothly rolling—places to climb with labor and places to gallop at ease. He saw streams that promised drink at will; he saw clumps and groves of trees for shelter from sun or storm. All that a horse could will was here, beyond imaginings. Alcatraz lifted his beautiful head and neighed across the lowlands.

There was no answer. His kingdom silently awaited his coming so he struck out at a sharp pace. The run of the day before, in place of stiffening him, had put him in racing trim and he went like the wind. He was in playful mood. He danced and shied as each cloud-shadow struck him, a dim figure in the shade but shining red-chestnut in the sun patches. On every hand he saw dozens of places where he would have stopped willingly had not more distant beauties lured him on. There were hills whose tops would serve him as watch towers in time of need. There were meadows of soft soil where the grass grew long and rank and others where it was a sweeter and finer growth; but both had their places in his diet and must be remembered so Alcatraz tried to file them away in his mind. But who could remember single jewels in a great treasure? He was like a child chasing butterflies and continually lured from the pursuit of one to that of another still brighter. So he came in his kingly progress to the first blot on the landscape, the first bar, the first hindrance.

Sinuous and swift curving as a snake it twisted over hilltops and dipped across hollows, three streaks of silver light one above the other, and endless. The ears of Alcatraz flattened. He knew barb-wire fences of old and he knew they meant man and domination of man. The scars of whip and spur stung him afresh. The old sullen hatred rose in him. Those three elusive lines of light were stronger than he, he knew, just as the frail body of a man contained a mysterious strength far greater than his. He turned his head across the wind and galloped beside the new-strung fence for ten breathless minutes. Then he paused, panting. Still running endless before him and behind was the fence and now he saw a checking of similar fences across the meadows to his right. More than that, he saw a group of fat cattle browsing, and just beyond were horses in a pasture.

Alcatraz slipped backwards and sideways till he was out of sight and then galloped over the hill until he came to a grove of trees at the top. Here he paused to continue his examination from shelter. The fence was the work of man, the cattle and horses were the possessions of man, and far off to the left, out of a grove of trees, rose the smoke which spoke of the presence of man himself. The chestnut shivered as though he were shaking cold water off his hide, and then unreasoning fury gripped him. For here was his paradise, his Promised Land, pre-empted by the Great Enemy!

He stayed for a long moment gazing, and then turned reluctantly and fled like one pursued back by the way he had come. He got beyond the fence in the course of half an hour, but still he kept on. He began to feel that as long as he galloped on land which was pleasant to him it would be pleasant to man also. So he kept steadily on his way, leaping the brooks. Into the river he cast himself and swam to the farther shore. There was an instant change beyond that bank. The valley opened like a fan. The handle of it was the green, well-watered plateau into which he had first descended, but now it spread in raw colored desert, cut up by ragged hills here and there, and extending on either side to mountains purple-blue with distance.

With the water dripping from his belly, Alcatraz twinked a farewell glance to the green country behind him and set his face towards the desert. It was not so hard to leave the pleasant meadows. Now that he knew they were man-owned there was a taint in their beauty, and here on the sands of the desert with only dusty bunch-grass to eat and muddy waterholes to drink from, he was at least free from the horror of the enemy. He kept on fairly steadily, nibbling in the bunch-grass as he went, now trotting a little, now cantering lightly across a stretch barren of forage. So he came, just after noonday, down-wind from the scent of horses.

His own kind, yet he was worried, for he connected horses inevitably with the thought of man. Nevertheless, he decided to explore, and coming warily over a rise of ground he saw, in the hollow beyond, a whole troop of horses without a man in sight. He was too wise to jump to conclusions but slipped back from his watch-post and ran in a long semi-circle about the herd, but having made out that there was no cowpuncher nearby, he came back to his original place of vantage and resumed his observations.

A beautiful black stallion wandered up-wind from the rest and another, younger horse, was on the other side of the herd. Between was a raggedly assembled group of mares old and young, with leggy yearlings, deer-footed colts, and more than one time-worn stallion. It was a motley assembly. The colors ranged from piebald to grey and there was a great diversity in stature. Presently the black stallion neighed softly, whereat the rest of the herd bunched closely together, the mares with the foals on the side, and all heads turning towards the black who now galloped to a hilltop, surveyed the horizon and presently dropped his head to graze again.

This was a signal to the others. They spread out again carelessly, but Alcatraz was beginning to put two and two together in his thoughts. The two stallions were obviously guards, but what should they be guarding against in the broad light of day except that terrible destroyer who hunts as well at noon as at midnight—man! Inspiration came to Alcatraz. The difference of color and stature, the unkempt manes and tails, the wild eyes, were all telling a single story, now. These were not servants to man, and since they were not his servants they must be enemies, for that was the law of the world. The great enemy dominated, and where he could not dominate he killed. And the herd feared the same power which Alcatraz feared; instantly they became to him brothers and sisters, and he stepped boldly into view.

The result was startling. From the hilltop the black stallion whinnied shrill and short and in a twinkling the whole group was in motion scurrying north. Alcatraz looked in wonder and saw the black fall in behind the rest and range across the rear biting the flanks of older horses who found it difficult to keep the hot pace. With this accomplished and when the herd was stolidly compacted before his driving, the black skirted around the whole group and with a magnificent spurt of running placed himself in the lead. He kept his place easily, a strong galloping grey mare at his hip, and from time to time tossed his head to the side to take stock of his followers. And so they dipped out of sight beyond the next swell of ground.

Alcatraz recovered from his amazement to start in pursuit. This was a mystery worth solving. Moreover, the moment he made sure that these were not man-owned creatures they had become inexplicably dear to him and as they disappeared his heart grew heavy. His running gait carried him quickly in view. They had slackened in their flight a little but as he hove in sight again they took the alarm once more, the foals first rushing to the front and then the whole herd with flying manes and tails blown straight out.

It was a goodly sight to Alcatraz. Moreover, his heart leaped strangely, as it always did when he saw horses in full gallop. Perhaps they were striving to test his speed of foot before they admitted him to their company. In that case the answer was soon given. He sent his call after them, bidding them watch a real horse run, then overtook them in one dizzy burst of sprinting. His rush carried him not only up to them but among them. Two or three youngsters swerved aside with frightened snorts, but as he came up behind a laboring mare she paused in her flight to let drive with both heels. Alcatraz barely escaped the danger with a sidestep light as a dancer's and shortened his gallop.

He could not punish the mare for her impudence; besides, he needed time to rearrange his thoughts. Why should they flee from a companion who intended no harm? It was a great puzzle. In the meantime, keeping easily at the heels of the wild horses, he noted that they were holding their pace better than any cowponies he had ever seen running. From the oldest mare to the youngest foal they seemed to have one speed afoot.

A neigh from the black leader made the herd scatter on every side like fire in stubble. Alcatraz halted to catch the meaning of this new maneuver and saw the black approaching at a high-stepping trot as one determined to explore a danger but ready to instantly flee if it seemed a serious threat. His gaze was fixed not on Alcatraz but on the far horizon where the hills became a blue mist rolling softly against the sky. He seemed to make up his mind, presently, that nothing would follow the chestnut out of the distance and he began to move about Alcatraz in a rapid gallop, constantly narrowing his circle.

Alcatraz turned constantly to meet him, whinnying a friendly greeting, but the black paid not the slightest heed to these overtures. At length he came to a quivering stand twenty yards away, head up, ears back, a very statue of an angry and proud horse. Obviously it was a challenge, but Alcatraz was too happy in his new-found brothers to think of battle. He ducked his head a little and pawed the ground lightly, a horse's age-old manner of expressing amicable intentions. But there was nothing amicable in the black leader. He reared a little and came down lightly on his forefeet, his weight gathered on his haunches as though he were preparing to charge, and at this unmistakable evidence of ill-will, Alcatraz snorted and grew alert.

If it came to fighting he was more than at home. He was a master. More than one corral gate he had cunningly worked ajar, and more than one flimsy barn wall he had broken down with his leaning shoulder, and more than one fence he had leaped to get at the horses beyond. With anger rising in him he took stock of the opponent. The black lacked a good inch of his own height but in substance more than made up for the deficiency. He was a stalwart eight-year old, muscled like a Hercules, with plenty of bone to stand his weight; and his eyes, glittering through the tangle of forelock, gave him an air of savage cunning. Decidedly here was a foeman worthy of his steel, thought Alcatraz. He looked about him. There stood the mares and the horses ranged in a loose semi-circle, waiting and watching; only the colts, ignorant of what was to come, had begun to frolic together or bother their mothers with a savage pretense of battle. Alcatraz saw one solid old bay topple her offspring with a side-swing of her head. She wanted an unobstructed view of the fight.

His interest in this by-play nearly proved his undoing for while his head was turned he heard a rushing of hoofs and barely had time to throw himself to one side as the black flashed by him. Alcatraz turned and reared to beat the insolent stranger into the earth but he found that the leader was truly different from the sluggish horses of men. A hundred wild battles had taught the black every trick of tooth and heel; and in the thick of the fight he carried his weight with the agility of a cat: Alcatraz had not yet swung himself fairly back on his haunches when the black was upon him, the dust flying up behind from the quickness of his turn. Straight at the throat of the chestnut he dived and his teeth closed on the throat of Alcatraz just where the neck narrows beneath the jaw. His superior height enabled Alcatraz to rear and fling himself clear, but his throat was bleeding when he landed on all fours dancing with rage and the sting of his wounds. Yet he refrained from rushing; he had been in too many a fight to charge blindly.

The black, however, had tasted victory, and came again with a snort of eagerness. It was the thing for which Alcatraz had been waiting and he played a trick which he had learned long before from a cunning old gelding who, on a day, had given him a bitter fight. He pitched back, as though he were about to rear to meet the charge, but when his fore-feet were barely clear of the ground he rocked down again, whirled, and lashed out with his heels.

Had they landed fairly the battle would have ended in that instant, but the black was cat-footed indeed, and he swerved in time to save his head. Even so one flashing heel had caught his shoulder and ripped it open like a knife. And they both sprang away, ready for the next clash. The grey mare who had run so gallantly at the hip of the leader now approached and stood close by with pricking ears. Alcatraz bared his teeth as he glanced aside at her. No doubt if he were knocked sprawling she would rush in to help her lord and master finish the enemy. That gave Alcatraz a second problem—to fight the stallion without turning his back on the treacherous mare.

Before he could plan his next move the black was at him again. This time they reared together, met with a clash of teeth and rapid beat of hoofs, and parted on equal terms. Alcatraz eyed his enemy with a fierce respect. His head was dull and ringing with the blows; his shoulder had been slightly cut by a glancing forehoof. Decidedly he could not meet the brawn of this hardened old warrior on such terms. He had used up one trick, he must find another, and still another; and when the black rushed again, Alcatraz slipped away from the contact and raced off at his matchless gallop. The other pursued a short distance and stopped, sounding his defiance and his triumph. As well follow the wind as the chestnut stranger. Besides, the blood was pouring from the gash in his shoulder and that foreleg was growing weak; it was well that the battle had ended at this point.

But it was not ended! Flight was not in the mind of Alcatraz as he swept away. He ran in dodging circles about the enemy, swerving in and then veering sharply out as the black reared to meet the expected charge. Whatever else was accomplished, he had gained the initiative and that plus his lightness of foot might bring matters to a decisive issue in his favor. Twice he made his rush; twice the black turned and met him with that shower of crushing blows with the fore hoofs. But the third time a feint at one side and a charge at the other took the leader unawares. Fair and true the shoulder of Alcatraz struck him on the side and the impact flung the black heavily to the earth. The shock had staggered even Alcatraz but he was at the other like a savage terrier. Thrice he stamped across that struggling body until the black lay motionless with his coat crimson from twenty slashes. Then Alcatraz drew away and neighed his triumph, and in his exultation he noted that the herd drew close together at his call.

Why, he could not imagine, and he had no time to ponder on it, for the black was now struggling to his feet. But there was no fight left in him. He stood dazed, with fallen head, and to the challenge of the chestnut he replied by not so much as the pricking of his flagging ears.

The grey mare went to him, touched noses with her overlord, and then backed away, shaking her head. Presently she trotted past Alcatraz, flung up her heels within an inch of his head, and then galloped on towards the herd looking back at the conqueror. Oh vanity of the weaker sex; oh frailty! She had seen her master crushed and within the minute she was flirting with the conqueror.

The herd started off as the grey joined them and Alcatraz followed; the black leader remaining unmoving and the blood dripped steadily down his legs.

CHAPTER VIII
MURDER

AFTER they had seen him in battle it seemed to Alcatraz that there might be some reason for the flight of the herd and yet now their running was only half-hearted; he could have raced in circles around them. There was one change in their arrangement. The grey mare was second, as before, but before her in place of the black ran the bay stallion who had stood down—wind from the rest when Alcatraz first saw them. He, perhaps, might challenge the stranger as the former leader had done. At any rate he should have the opportunity, for the fighting blood of Alcatraz was up and he would battle with every horse in the herd until he was accepted among them as an equal. He had a peculiar desire, also, to be up there beside the grey mare. Their meeting had been, indeed, only in the passing, and yet there was about her—how should one say?—a certain something.

The moment he had made up his mind, Alcatraz flung himself about the herd and advanced with high head and bounding gallop on the new leader; but the latter had seen his former master fall and apparently had no appetite for battle. He shortened his pace to a hand gallop, then to a mincing trot, and finally lowered his head and moved unobtrusively to the side with an absorbed interest in the first knot of bunch-grass that came his way. To force battle on such a foe was beneath the dignity of Alcatraz, but the whole herd had stopped, every bright eye watching him; perhaps there might be others more ambitious than the bay. He put up his head like the king of horses that he was and stepped proudly forward. Behold, they divided and left a clear path before him; even the mare who had kicked at him when he first came up now shook her head and moved aside. He reached the rear of the herd unopposed and turned to find that every head was still turned towards him with a bright attention that was certainly not altogether fear.

This was very strange, and while he thought it over Alcatraz dropped his head and nibbled the nearest cluster of grass. At that, as at a signal, every head in the herd went down; it scattered carelessly here and there. Alcatraz watched them, bewildered. This was what he had noted when the black leader was among them; then he understood and was filled with warm content. Truly they had accepted him not only as a member but as a master! To prove it, he trotted to the nearest hilltop and neighed as he had heard the black neigh. At once they bunched, looking warily towards him. He lowered his head to nibble the grass and again they scattered to eat. It was true. It was true beyond shadow of doubt that from this moment he was a king with obedient subjects until, perhaps, some younger, mightier stallion challenged and beat him down. Happily for Alcatraz such forethought was beyond his reach of mind and now he only knew the happiness of power.

He noticed a long-bodied colt, incredibly dainty of foot, wandering nervously near him with pricking ears and sniffing nose. Alcatraz extended his lordly head and sniffed the velvet muzzle, whereat the youngster snorted and darted away shaking his head and kicking up his heels as though he had just bearded the lion and was delighted at the success of his impertinence. The mother had come anxiously close during this adventure but now she regarded Alcatraz with a friendly glance and went about her serious business of eating for two.

The grey mare was drifting near, likewise, as though by inadvertence, nibbling the headed grasstops as she came; but Alcatraz shrewdly guessed that her approach was not altogether unplanned. He was not displeased. His quiet happiness grew as the cloud—shadows rushed across him and the sun warmed him. It was a pleasant world—a pleasant, pleasant world! His people wandered in the hollow. They looked to him for warning of danger. They looked at him for guidance in a crisis and he accepted the burden cheerfully.

Fear, it seemed, had made him one with them. All his life he had dreaded only one thing—man; but these creatures of the wild had many a fear of the lobo, the mountain-lion, the drought, the high flying buzzard who would claim them, dying, and added above all this, man. Not that Alcatraz knew these things definitely. He could only feel that these, his people, were strong only in their speed and in their timidity, and he felt power to rule and protect them. For he who had fought man, and won, had surely nothing to dread from beasts. The great moment of his life had come to him not in the crushing of the Mexican or the baffling of the mountain lion or the defeat of the black leader but in the first gentle kindness that had ever softened his stern spirit. He was used to battle; but these, his people, accepted him. He was used to suspicion and trickery but these trusted him blindly. He was used to hate, but because they had put themselves into his power he began to love them. He felt a blood-tie between him and the weakest colt within the range of his eye.

The herd drifted slowly down—wind until late afternoon, eating their way rather than travelling, but when the heat began to wane and the slant sunlight took on a yellow tone they began to show signs of unrest, milling in a compact group with the foals frolicking on the outskirts of the circle. The mares were particularly disturbed, it seemed to Alcatraz, especially the mothers; and since all heads were turned repeatedly towards him he became anxious. Something was expected of him. What was it?

In case they had scented a danger unknown to him, he cast a wide circle around them at a sharp gallop, but nothing met his nostril, his eye, or his ear except the dust with its keen taint of alkali, and the bare hills, and the vague horizon sounds. Alcatraz came back to his companions at a halting trot which denoted his uneasy alertness. They were milling more closely than ever. The brood mares had passed to a sullen nervousness and were kicking savagely at everything that came near. Decidedly something was wrong. The wise-headed grey mare loped out to meet him and threw a course of circles around him as he came slowly forward. Plainly she expected him to do something, but what this might be Alcatraz could not tell. Besides, a growing thirst was making him irritable and the insistence of the grey mare made him wish to fasten his teeth over the back of her neck and shake her into better behavior.

By her antics she had worked him around to the head of the herd and she had no sooner reached this point than she threw up her head with a shrill neigh and started off at a gallop. The entire herd rushed after her and Alcatraz, in a bound, ranged along side the grey and a neck in the lead. While he ran he whinnied a soft question to which she replied with a toss of her head as though impatient at such ignorance. In reality she was guiding the herd. She knew it and Alcatraz understood her knowledge, but he made a show of maintaining the guidance, keeping a sharp outlook and turning the moment she showed signs of veering in a new direction. Sometimes, of course, he misread her intentions and swerved across her head and on each of these occasions she reached out and nipped him shrewdly. Alcatraz was too taken up in his wonder at the actions of the herd to resent this insolence. For half an hour they kept up the steady pace and then Alcatraz literally ran into the reason.

It was a beautiful little lake, bedded in hard gravel and maintained by a dribble of water from a brook on the north shore. Alcatraz snorted in disgust at his folly. What had disturbed them was exactly what had disturbed him—thirst. He controlled his own desire for water, however, and followed an instinct that made him draw back and wait until all the rest—the oldest stallion and the youngest colt—had waded in and plunged their noses deep in the water. Then he went to the lake edge a little apart from the rest and drank with his reflection glistening beneath him.

It was a time of utter peace for the chestnut. While he drank he watched the line of images broken by the small waves in the lake and listened to the foals which had only tasted the water and now were splashing it about with their upper lips. For his own part he did not drink too much, since much water in the belly makes a leaden burden and Alcatraz felt that, as leader, he must always be ready for running. A scrawny colt, escaping from the heels of a yearling floundered against him. Alcatraz gave way to the little fellow and warned the yearling back with a savage baring of his teeth and a shake of his head. The foal, with head cocked upon one side, regarded its protector with impish curiosity and was in the act of nibbling at the flowing mane of the stallion when Alcatraz heard a sharp humming as of a wasp; then the sound of a blow, and the foal leaped straight into the air with head flung back. Before it hit water a report as of a hammer falling on anvil burst across the level pond, and then the colt struck heavily on its side, dead.

That bullet had been aimed for the tall leader and only the lifting of the foal's head had saved Alcatraz. He recognized the report of a rifle and whirled from the water-edge, signalling his company with a short neigh of fear; the arch enemy was upon them! A volley poured in. Alcatraz, as he gained the shore, saw an old stallion double up with a scream of pain and no sound is so terrible as the shriek of a tortured horse. No sound is so terrible even to horses. It threw the leader into an hysteria of panic. Others of the herd were falling or staggering in the lake; the remnant rushed up the slope and over the sheltering crest of the hill beyond.

Every nerve in the body of Alcatraz urged him to leap away with arrowy speed, passing even the grey mare—she who now shot off across the hills far in the van—but behind him raced weaker and slower horses, the older stallions and the mares with their foals. Instinct proved greater than fear. He swept around the rear of his diminished company to round up the laggards, but they were already laboring to the full of their power as five horsemen streamed across the crest with their rifles carried at the ready. They were a hardy crew, these cowpunchers of the Jordan ranch, but to the sternest of them this was ugly work. To draw a bead on a horse was like gathering the life of a man into the sight of the rifle, yet they knew that a band of wildrunning mustangs is a perpetual menace. Already the black leader had recruited his herd with more than one stray from the Jordan outfit; and it was for the black, first of all, that they looked. There was no sign of him, and in his place ranged a picture horse— a beautiful red—chestnut with a gallop that made one's head swim. Lew Hervey, who had kept his men in cunning ambush near the lake, had chosen the new leader for a target but shot the colt instead. And it was Lew Hervey, again, who swung over the crest of the hill and got the next chance at Alcatraz.

The foreman of the Jordan ranch pitched his rifle to his shoulder just as the leader, sweeping back to round up the rearmost of his company, presented a broadside target. It was a sure hit. In the certainty of his skill Lew Hervey allowed his hand to swing and followed for a strike or two the rhythm of that racing body. The sunshine of the late afternoon flashed on the flanks and on the frightened eyes of the stallion; mane and tail fluttered straight out with his speed; and then he fired, and jerked up his gun to await the crashing fall of the horse. But Alcatraz did not drop. That moment of lingering on the part of the foreman saved him, for through the sights of his rifle Hervey had seen such grace and beauty in horseflesh that his nerve was unsteadied. Alcatraz knew the stinging hum of a bullet past his head; and the foreman knew a miracle. He could not believe his failure.

"Leave the chestnut to me!" he shouted as his men drove their ponies over the hill, and pulling his own horse to a stand he jerked the rifle butt hard against his shoulder and fired again; the only result was a flirt of the tail of the chestnut as he darted about a hillside and disappeared. Hervey made no attempt to follow but sat his saddle agape and staring, thinking ghostly thoughts.

This was the beginning of the legend that Alcatraz bore a charmed life. For the mountains were rich with Indian folklore which had drifted far from its source and had come by hook and crook into the lives of the miners and cowpunchers. Into such a background many a wild tale fitted and the tale of Alcatraz was to be one of the wildest.

At any rate, the stallion owed his life on this day to the superstition of Lew Hervey which kept him anchored on his horse until the target was gone. A dozen times his men could have dropped the chestnut who persisted with a frantic courage in running behind the rearmost of his companions, urging them to greater efforts, but since Hervey had selected this as his own prize his men dared not shoot.

It was a strange and beautiful thing to see that king of horses—sweep back around the slowest of his mustangs, shake his head at the barking guns, and then circle forward again as though he would show the laggard what running should be. The cowpunchers could have shot him as he veered back; they could have salted him with lead as he flashed broadside, but the orders of their chief restrained them. Lew Hervey's lightest word had a weight with them.

However, before and behind the leader of the herd their guns did deadly work. Brood mares, stallions young and old, even the foals were dropped. It was horrible work to the hardest of them but this horseflesh was useless. Too many times they had seen mustangs taken and ridden and when they were not hopeless outlaws they became broken-spirited and useless, as though their strength lay in their freedom. With that gone they were valueless even as slaves of men.

Before the slaughter ended, young or old there was not a horse left in the band of Alcatraz save the grey mare far ahead. She was already beyond range, and as the last of the fleeing horses pitched heavily forward and lay still with oddly sprawling limbs, old Bud Seymour drew rein and shoved his rifle back into the long holster.

"Now, look!" he called, as his companions pulled up beside him. "That grey is fast as a streak—but look! look!"

For the red-chestnut was bounding away in pursuit of his last companion with a winged gallop. It seemed that the wind caught him up and buoyed him from stride to stride, and the cowpunchers with hungry, burning eyes watched without a word until the grey and the chestnut blurred on the horizon and dipped out of view together. The spell was broken in the same instant by a stream of profanity floating up from the rear. It was Lew Hervey approaching and swearing his mightiest.

"But I dunno," said Bud Seymour softly. "I feel kind of glad that Lew missed."

He glanced sharply at his companions for fear they might laugh at this childish weakness, but there was no laughter and by their starved eyes he knew that every one of them was riding over the horizon in imagination, on the back of the chestnut.

CHAPTER IX
THE STAMPEDE

THE grey mare made no effort to draw away when Alcatraz sprinted up beside her. She gave him not so much as a toss of the head or a swish of the tail but kept her gaze on the far Western mountains for she was still sick with the scent of blood; and she maintained a purposeful, steady, lope. It was far other with the stallion. He kept at her side with his gliding canter but he was not thinking of the peace and the shelter from man which they might find in the blue valleys of yonder mountains. His mind was back at the slaughter of Mingo Lake hearing the crackle of the rifles and seeing his comrades fall and die. It was nothing that he had known the band only since morning. They were his kind, they were his people, they had accepted his rule; and now he was emptyhearted, a king without a people. The grey mare, the fleetest and the wisest of them all, remained; but she was only a reminder of his vanished glory.

Remembering how Cordova had been served, might he not find a way of harming those men even as they had harmed him? He slackened to a trot and finally halted. His companion kept on until he neighed. Then she came obediently enough but swinging her head up and down to indicate her intense disapproval of this halt. When Alcatraz actually started back towards the place where the cowpunchers had dropped the pursuit, she threw herself across his way, striving to turn him with bared teeth and flirting heels.

He merely kept a weaving course to avoid her, his head high and his ears back, which was a manner the mare had never seen in him before; she could only tell that she was less than nothing to him. Once she strove to draw back by running a little distance west and then turning and calling him but her whinny made him not so much as shake his head. At length she surrendered and sullenly took up his trail.

He roved swiftly across the hollows; he sneaked up to every commanding rise as though he feared the guns of men might be just beyond the crest and these tactics continued until they came in view of the small row of black figures riding against the sunset. The grey halted at once, rearing and snorting, for the sight brought again that hateful smell of blood but her leader moved quietly after the cowpunchers; he was taking the man-trail!

It was arduous work, frisking from one point of vantage to another, never knowing when the Great Enemy might turn. They could make death speak from the distance of half a mile; under shelter of the hills they might even double back to close range; they might be luring him by the pretense that he was unseen.

In such maneuvers the mare was a dangerous encumbrance, for though she had fallen into the spirit of the thing at once and never uttered even the faintest whinny yet it would be far easier for the men to hear and see two than to detect one. Alcatraz strove to drive her back, sometimes whirling with teeth bared and rushing at her, sometimes halfrearing as though to strike. But on such occasions she merely stopped and regarded him with eyes of mild amazement. She knew perfectly that he would never touched her with tooth or hoof; she also knew that this was dangerous folly—this badgering of terrible man, but since Alcatraz was not wise enough to follow her she must even follow him in spite of his folly.

She stayed half a dozen lengths in the rear, trembling with excitement, for now they passed the verge of the desert and now they entered a man-made road bordered with shining fences of men; what retreat was there if men closed in from the front and the rear? Yet she went on with dainty and uneasy steps. As for Alcatraz, he had pressed up boldly, close to the riders, for now the twilight grew thick and it was hard to make out the glimmering forms before him. Twice he paused; twice he went on. There was no real purpose in this following. He dared not come too close, and yet he hoped to harm them. He continued, wrung by a confusion of dreads and desires.

He was beset with signs of man even in the darkness. Over the well-watered fields of the ranch he heard the lowing of cattle and now and again the chorus of the sheep in a nearby pasture land was reawakened when the bell of the leader tinkled. They were all hateful sounds to Alcatraz, and every step he made seemed to consign him the more definitely to the power of the Great Enemy.

In spite of his boldness he lost sight of the riders among the deeper shadows of the ranch buildings, and he stopped again to consider. The grey mare came beside him and begged him back with a call softer than a whisper, but he merely raised his head the higher and stared at the huge outlines of the sheds and barns. To Alcatraz every one of them was a fortress filled with danger that might leap up at him. Yet he must not turn back after having come all this distance, surely. He went on. The road opened into an unfenced semicircle with corrals on every side and from one of these enclosures a horse neighed, and there was a brief sound of many trampling feet. Some of his own kind were playing there; Alcatraz forgot his hatred a little, forgot man. He went straight to the corral and put his head over the top bar.

Snorting softly, curious and frightened at once, six beautiful animals came towards him. He was one of their kind, so they came close; the scent of the wilderness was already on him, and they shrank away. Surely some sinister genius had directed Alcatraz to the one most valuable point of attack on all the ranch, for these were the six brood mares for whose purchase Marianne Jordan had cleaned out her bank account. The stallion did not know, of course. He did not even recognize them as his competitors in the race. All he felt was that there was something charmingly remembered, something half familiar about them. The boldest came near and he touched noses, whereat she whirled with a little squeal and lashed out at him; but her heels were carefully aimed wide of the mark and Alcatraz merely tossed his nose; plainly she was a flirt. He pressed a little closer to the fence and urged friendliness with a conversational whinny. They were not averse, coming towards him with eyes that glimmered in the darkness, retreating often and coming on again, until he had touched noses with them all. It was extremely pleasant to Alcatraz and hardly less so because the grey mare came and shouldered him rudely.

Then a voice spoke from the barn which opened off the corral: "What's all that damned nonsense with the mares yonder?"

Alcatraz crouched for flight. Another voice answered: "They'll mill around every night for a while till they get used to the new place. That's the way with them crazy hot-bloods. No hoss-sense."

The voices departed. The shrinking of the stallion had made the mares wince away in turn, but they came back now and resumed the conversation where it had been broken off. He was careful to introduce himself to each one. He was greatly tempted to jump the fence and talk to them at closer hand but he knew that it was great folly to risk his neck in a group of mares before he had made out whether or not they were amiable. If they were cross-tempered he might be kicked to death before he could escape.

The investigations brought entirely favorable returns. They were very young, these Coles horses, and hence their curiosity was far stronger than their timidity. Before long every one of the six necks was stretched across the top-rail and when Alcatraz turned his back on them they whinnied uneasily to call him back.

If that were the case, why did they not jump? He went back and showed them how simple it was if they really wanted to escape and come out with him into the wind and under the free stars of the mountains. Such a fence was nothing to that powerful jumper. He walked calmly to it, reared, and sailed over. That sent the mares scampering wildly, here and there about the corral, and though they came back again after a time, they seemed to have learned nothing. When he jumped out again not one of them followed.

Alcatraz stood off and eyed them in disgust. When he was a yearling, he felt, he had known more than those big, stupid, beautiful creatures. But plainly they wanted to get out with him. A wild horse is to the tame what the adventurous traveller is to the quiet man who builds a home, and from the grey mare and Alcatraz the six were learning many things. The scent of the open desert was on them, the sweat of hard running had dried on their hides, their heads were recklessly proud; and this tall stallion jumped the fence as though there had never been men who made laws which well-trained horses must not transgress. Plainly he wanted them to come out. They were very willing to go for a romp but they knew nothing about jumping, as yet, and all they could do was to show their eagerness to be out for a run by milling up and down the fence.

If that were the case, there were other ways of opening corrals and Alcatraz knew them all. He tried the fence with his shoulder, leaning all his weight. More than once he had smashed time-rotted fences in this manner, but he found that these posts were new and well tamped and the boards were strongly nailed. He gave up that effort and went about looking for a gate. Gates were not hard to find. A gate is that part of a fence under which many tracks and many scents go; it is also a section which swings a little and rattles annoyingly in a wind. Upon the top board of that section there is sure to be thick scent of man where his hands have fallen. Alcatraz found the gate. Under the weight of his shoulder it creaked but did not give. He took the top rail in his teeth, while the mares stood back, wondering, in a high-headed semi-circle and the grey kept nudging at his flank, saying very plainly: "Enough of this nonsense. These gangling creatures, all legs and foolishness, are not of our kind, O my master. Let us be gone!" But

Alcatraz heeded her not. He shook the gate back and forth.

There are three kinds of fastenings for corral gates. One of them squeaks and strains when it is pulled against. It is made of wire that leaves a bitter taste of iron and rust in the mouth when it is touched. Wire is often very difficult but with teeth and prehensile upper lip it may usually be worked up high, and finally it will fall over the top of one of the posts with a rattle, and then the gate is open. Another kind of fastening rattles very much when the gate is shaken. This means that a loose board unites gates and post, running in a slot, and the only way to handle such a gate is to take the loose board by the end and draw it back as far as possible. Then the gate always swings open of its own accord. There is a third kind of fastening. Manuel Cordova used it. It consists of a padlock and chain and where this is found one had better leave the cursed thing untried for it will never be broken or removed.

By the first shake of the gate and the corresponding rattle Alcatraz knew that the sliding board fastened it. He sniffed for it and found it very easily, for always the latch-board is the one heaviest with the man-scent. He found it and worked it easily back. It caught on a nail. He tugged again, and as he tugged he quivered at the sound of a human voice and shrank as though the familiar whip of Cordova had cut him.

"They're a little restless to-night, but aren't they dears, Shorty?" queried Marianne.

"Kind of dear," said the cowpuncher, "but maybe they're worth the price." For all his surliness, however, Shorty was her best ally.

"Wait till you see Lady Mary begin to—but isn't that a horse beyond the corral? A grey horse? I think it is, but it can't be."

"Why not?"

"There isn't a grey horse on the ranch, and—oh!"

For the gate of the corral creaked and then swung wide. They could not see Alcatraz, for the bay mares stood between.

"Don't move, don't speak!" whispered the girl. "It's that stupid Lucas man. I told Lew Hervey that he was too careless to take care of the mares; and the first thing he's done is to leave the gate unlatched. I'll steal around and—"

At the first sound of the voice the grey mare had drifted deeper into the safety of the night; Alcatraz with a careful effort pulled open the gate; and the wind, aiding him, blew it wide, and now the soft whinny of invitation to the mares cut into the words of Marianne. She went around the corral bending low, skulking in her run; for once the mares got out the gate they might bolt like crazy things and come to harm in the murderous barbed-wire fences. Shorty was hurrying around on the other side.

Before she had taken half a dozen steps the neigh of the stallion, deafeningly loud, brought her to a halt with her hands clasped. She saw the mares start under the alarm-call and rush for the gate; in a moment their hoofs were volleying down the road and the wail of Marianne went shrilling: "Lew Hervey! Lew Hervey! They're gone!"

Lew Hervey, in the bunkhouse, pushed away his cards and rose with a curse.

"That's what comes of working for a woman," he growled. "No peace. No rest. Work day and night. And if you ain't kept working you're just kept worried. It's hell!"

He clumped to the door and cast it open.

"Well?" he called into the darkness.

"Every one out!" cried Marianne. "The mares have broken through the gate and stampeded!"

CHAPTER X
THE THIEF

THEY came with a rush, at that. The mares the girl prized so highly were, in the phrase of the cowpunchers, "high-headed fools" incapable of taking care of themselves. Running wild through the night, as likely as not they would cut themselves to pieces on the first barbed wired fence that blocked their way. With such a thought to urge them, Marianne's hired men caught their fastest mounts and saddled like lightning. There was a play of ropes and curses in the big corral, the scuffle of leather as saddle after saddle flopped into place, and then a stream of dim riders darted through the corral gate.

All of this, dazed by the misfortune, Marianne waited to see, but as the first of the pursuers darted out of sight she turned and ran to the box stall where she kept her favorite pony, a nimble bay, inimitable on a mountain trail and with plenty of foot on the flat. But never did hurry waste so much precious time. The rush of her entrance in the dark startled the nervous horse, and she had to soothe it for a minute or more with a voice broken by excitement. After that, there was the saddling to be done and her fingers stumbled and stuttered over the straps so that when at last she led the bay out and swung up to the saddle there was no sound or sight of the cowpunchers. But a young moon was edging above the eastern mountains and by that light, now only an illusory haze, she hoped to gain sight of her men.

Down the road she jockeyed the mare at the top of her pace with the barbed wire running in three dim streaks of light on either side until at last she struck the edge of the desert. The moon was now well above the horizon and the sands rolled in dun levels and black hollows over which she could peer for a considerable distance. Still there was no sight of her cowpunchers and this was a matter of small wonder, for a ten minute start had sent them far away ahead of her.

It would never do to push ahead with a blind energy. Already the bay was beginning to feel the run, and Marianne reluctantly drew down to the long lope which is the favorite gait of the cowpony. At this pace she rocked on over mile after mile of desert through the moonhaze, but never a token of the cowpunchers came on her. Twice she was on the verge of turning back; twice she shook her head and urged the mare on again. Hour upon hour had slipped by her. Perhaps Hervey long since had given up the chase and turned towards the ranch. In the meantime, so much alike was all the ground she covered that she seemed to be riding on a treadmill but yet she could not return.

The moon floated higher and higher as the night grew old and at length there was a dim lightening in the east which foretold dawn, but Marianne kept on. If she lost the mares it would be very much like losing her last claim to the respect of her father. She could see him, in prospect, shrug his shoulders and roll another cigarette; above all she could see Lew Hervey smile with a suppressed wisdom. Both of them had, from the first, not only disapproved of the long price of the Coles horses, but of their long legs as well and their "damned high heads." She had kept telling herself fiercely that before long, when the mares were used to mountain ways and trails, she would ride one of them against the pick of Hervey's saddle ponies and at the end of a day he would know how much blood counts in horse flesh! But if that chance were lost to her with the mares themselves—she did not know where she could find the courage to go back and face the people at the ranch. Meantime the dawn grew slowly in the east but even when the mountains were huge and black against flaming colors of the horizon sky, there was no breaking of Marianne's gloom. Now and then, hopelessly, she raised her field glasses and swept a segment of the compass. But it was an automatic act, and her own forecast of failure obscured her vision, until at last, saddle-racked, trembling with weariness and grief, she stopped the mare. She was beaten!

She had turned the bay towards the home-trail when something subconsciously noted made her glance over her shoulder. And she saw them! She needed no glass to bring them close. Those six small forms moving over the distant hill could be nothing else, but if she doubted, all room for doubt was instantly removed, for in a moment a group of horsemen passed raggedly over the same crest. Hervey had found them, after all! Tears of relief and astonishment streamed down her face. God bless Lew Hervey for this good work!

Even the bay seemed to recover her spirit at the sight. She had picked up her head before she felt the rein of the mistress and now she answered the first word by swinging into a brisk gallop that overhauled the others swiftly. How the eyes of Marianne feasted on the reclaimed truants! They danced along gaily, their slender bodies shining with sweat in the light of the early day, and Lady Mary mincing in the lead. A moment later, Marianne was among her cowpunchers.

They were stolid as ever but she knew them well enough to understand by the smiles they interchanged, that they were intensely pleased with their work of the night. Then she found herself crying to Hervey: "You're wonderful! Simply wonderful! How could you have followed them so far and found them in the night?"

At that, of course, Hervey became exceedingly matter of fact. He spoke as though the explanation were self-evident.

"They busted away in a straight line," he said, "so I knew by that that something was leading 'em. Them bays ain't got sense enough of their own to run so straight." She noted the slur without anger. "Well, what was leading 'em must of been what let 'em out of the corral; and what let 'em out of the corral—"

"Horse thieves!" cried Marianne, but Hervey observed her without interest.

"Hoss stealing ain't popular around these parts for some time," he said. "Rustle a cow, now and then, but they don't aim no higher—not since we strung Josh Sinclair to the cottonwood. Nope, they was stole, but not by a man."

Here he made a tantalizing pause to roll a cigarette with Marianne exclaiming: "If not a man, then what on earth, Mr. Hervey?"

He puffed out his answer with the first big cloud of smoke: "By another hoss! I guessed it right off. Remember what I said last night about the chestnut stallion and the bad luck he put on my gun?"

She recalled vividly how Hervey, with the utmost solemnity, had avowed that the leader of the mustangs put "bad luck" on his bullets and that they had not seen the last of the horse. She dared not trust herself to answer Lew but glanced at the other men to see if they were not smiling at their foreman's absurd idea; they were as grave as images.

"The chestnut wanted to get back at us for killing his herd off," went on Hervey. "So he sneaks up to the ranch and opens the corral gate and takes the mares out. When I seen the mares were traveling so straight as all that I guessed what was up. Well, if the hoss was leading 'em, where would he take 'em? Straight to water. They was no use trying to run down them long-legged gallopers. I took a swing off to the right and headed for Warner's Tank. Sure enough, when we got there we seen the mares spread out and the chestnut and the grey mare hanging around."

He paused again and looked sternly at Slim, and Slim flushed to the eyes and glared straight ahead.

"Slim, here, had been saying maybe it was my bum shooting and not the bad luck the stallion put on my rifle that made me miss. So I give him the job of plugging the hoss. Well, he tried and missed three times. Off goes the grey and the chestnut like a streak the first crack out of the box, but we got ahead of the mares and turned 'em. And here we are. That's all they was to it. But," he added gravely, "we ain't seen the last of that chestnut hoss, Miss Jordan."

"I guess hardly another man on the range could have trailed them so well," she said gratefully. "But this wild horse—do you really think he'll try to steal our mares again?"

"Think? I know! And the next time we won't get 'em back so plumb easy. Right this morning, if they'd got started quick enough when he give 'em the signal, we'd never of headed 'em. But they ain't turned wild yet; they ain't used to his ways. Give him another whirl with them and they'll belong to him for good. Ain't no hosses around these parts can run them mares down!"

She heard the tribute with a smile of pleasure and ran satisfied glances over the six beauties which cantered or trotted before them.

"But even wild things are captured," she argued. "Even deer are caught. If the chestnut *did* run off the mares again why couldn't—"

Hervey interrupted dryly: "Down Concord way, Jess Rankin was pestered by a black mustang. Jess was a pretty tolerable fair hunter, knowed mustangs and mustang-ways, and had a right fine string of saddle hosses. Well, it took Jess four years of hard work to get the black. Up by Mexico Creek, Bud Wilkinson had a grey stallion that run amuck on his range. Took Bud nigh onto five years to get the grey. Well, I seen both the grey and the black, and I helped run 'em a couple of times. Well, Miss Jordan, when it come to running, neither of 'em was one-two-three beside this chestnut, and if it took five years to get in rifle range of 'em for a good shot, it'll take ten to get the chestnut. That's the way I figure!"

And as he ended, his companions nodded soberly.

"Plumb streak of light," they said. "Just nacheral crazy fool when it comes to running, that hoss is!"

And Marianne, for the first time truly appreciating how great was the danger from which the mares had been saved, sighed as she looked them over again, one by one. It had been a double triumph, this night's work. Not only were the mares retaken, but they had proved their speed and staying powers conclusively in the long run over the desert. Hervey himself began hinting, as they rode on, that he would like "to clap a saddle on that Lady Mary hoss, one of these days." In truth, her purchase was vindicated completely and Marianne fell into a happy dream of a ranch stocked with saddle horses all drawn from the blood of these neat-footed mares. With such horses to offer, she could pick and cull among the best "punchers" in the West.

Into the dream, appropriately enough, ran the neigh of a horse, long drawn and shrill of pitch, interrupted by a sudden burst of deep-throated curses from the riders. The six mares had come to a halt with their beautiful heads raised to listen, and on a far-off hill, Mary saw the signaler—a chestnut horse gleaming red in the morning light.

"It's him!" shouted Hervey. "The nervy devil has come back to give us a look. Shorty, take a crack at him!"

For that matter, every man in the party was whipping his rifle out of its holster as Mary raised her field glass hurriedly to study the stranger. She focused on him clearly at once and it was a startling thing to see the distant figure shoot suddenly close to her, distinct in every detail, and every detail an item of perfect beauty. She gasped her admiration and astonishment; mustang he might be, but the short line of the back above and the long line below, the deep set of the shoulders, the length of neck, the Arab perfection of head, would have allowed him to pass unquestioned muster among a group of thoroughbreds, and a picked group at that. He turned, at that instant, and galloped a short distance along the crest, neighing again, and then paused like an expectant dog, with one forefoot raised, a white-stockinged forefoot. Marianne gripped the glass hard and then dropped it. By the liquid smoothness of that gallop, by the white-stockinged forefoot, by something about his head, and above all by what she knew of his cunning, she had recognized Alcatraz. And where, in the first glimpse, she had been about to warn the men not to shoot this peerless beauty, she now dropped the glass with the memory of the trampling of Manuel Cordova rushing back across her mind.

"It's Alcatraz!" she cried. "It's that chestnut I told you of at Glosterville, Mr. Hervey. Oh, shoot and shoot to kill. He's a murderer— not a horse!"

That injunction was not needed. The rifle spoke from the shoulder of Shorty, but the stallion neither fell nor fled, and his challenging neigh rang faintly down to them.

"Mind the mares!" shrilled Marianne suddenly. "They're starting for him!!"

In fact, it seemed as though the report of the rifle had started the Coles horses towards their late companion They went forward at a high-stepping trot as horses will when their minds are not quite made up about their course. Now, in obedience to shouted orders from Hervey, the cowpunchers split into two groups and slipped away on either side to head the truants; Marianne herself, spurring as hard as she could after Hervey, heard the foreman groaning: "By God, d'you ever *see* a hoss stand up under gunfire like that?"

For as they galloped, the men were pumping in shot after shot wildly, and Alcatraz did not stir! The firing merely served to rouse the mares from trot to gallop, and from gallop to run. For the first time Marianne mourned their speed. They glided away as though the horses of the cowpunchers were running fetlock deep in mud; they shot up the slope towards the distant stallion like six bright arrows.

Then came Hervey's last, despairing effort: "Pull up! Shorty! Slim! Pull up and try to drop that devil!"

They obeyed; Marianne, racing blindly ahead, heard a clanguor of shots behind her and riveted her eyes on the chestnut, waiting for him to fall. But he did not fall. He seemed to challenge the bullets with his lordly head and in another moment he was wheeling with the mares about him. Even in her anguish, Marianne noted with a thrill of wonder that though the Coles horses were racing at the top of their speed, the stallion overtook them instantly and shot into the lead. For that matter, handicapped with a wretched ride, staggering weak from underfeeding, he had been good enough to beat them in Glosterville, and now he was transformed by rich pasture and glorious freedom.

The whole group disappeared, and when she reached the crest in turn, she saw them streaking far off, hopelessly beyond pursuit, and in the rear labored a grey mare, sadly outrun. Then, as she drew rein, with the mare heaving and swaying from exhaustion beneath her, she remembered the words of Lew Hervey: "It'll take ten years to get the chestnut!" Marianne dropped her face in her hands and burst into tears.

It was only a momentary surrender. When she turned back to join the downheaded men on the home-trail—for it was worse than useless to follow Alcatraz on such jaded horses—Marianne had rallied to continue the fight. Ten years to capture Alcatraz and the mares he led? She swept the forms of the cowpunchers with one of those all-embracing glances of which few great men and all excited women are capable. Yes, old age would capture Alcatraz before such men as these. For this trail there was needed a spirit as much superior to other men in tireless endurance and in speed as Alcatraz was superior to other horses. There was needed a man who stood among his fellows as Alcatraz had stood on the hillcrest, defiant, lordly, and free. And as the thought drove home in her, Marianne uttered a little cry of triumph. All in a breath she had it. Red Perris was the man!

But would he come? Yes, for the sake of such a battle as this he would journey to the end of the world and give his services for nothing.

CHAPTER XI
THE FAILURE

BEFORE noon Shorty, that lightweight and tireless rider, unwearied, to all appearance, by his efforts of that night, had started towards Glosterville with her letter to Perris, but it was not until the next day that she confessed what she had done to Hervey. Certainly he had done more than his share in his effort to get back the Coles horses and she had no wish to needlessly hurt his feelings by letting him know that the business was to be taken out of his hands and given into those of a more efficient worker. But Hervey surprised her by the complaisance with which he heard the tidings.

"Never in my life hung out a shingle as a hoss-catcher," he assured her. "He's welcome to the job. Me and the boys won't envy him none. It'll be a long trail and a tolerable lonely one, most like."

After that she settled down to wait with as great a feeling of security as though the mares were already safely back in the corral. If he came, the death-warrant of Alcatraz was as good as signed. But when the third day of waiting ended without bringing Shorty and Perris, as it should have done, the "if" began to assume greater proportions, and by late afternoon of the fourth day she had made up her mind that Perris was gone from Glosterville and that Shorty was on a wild goose chase after him. So great was her gloom that even her father, usually blind to all emotions around him, delayed a moment after he had been helped into his buckboard and stared thoughtfully down at her.

The habit had grown on Oliver Jordan of late. When the westering sun lost most of its heat and threw slant shadows and a yellow light over the mountains, Oliver would have a pair of ancient greys, patient as burros and hardly faster, hitched to a buckboard and then drive off into the evening and perhaps, long after the dinner hour. Only foul weather kept him in from these lonely jaunts on which he never took a companion. To Marianne they were a never-ending source of wonder and sorrow, for she saw her father slowly withdrawing himself from the life about him and dwelling in a gentle, uninterrupted melancholy. She met his stare, on this evening, with eyes clouded with tears.

Truly he had aged wonderfully in the past years.

The accident which robbed him of his physical freedom seemed, at the same time, to destroy all spirit of youth. Whether walking or sitting he was bowed. His eyes were dull. Beside his mouth and between his eyes deep lines gave a sad dignity to his expression. And though, as his cowpunchers swore, his hand was as swift to draw a gun as ever and his eye as steady on a target, he had gradually lost interest in even his revolvers. Indeed, what real interest remained to him in the world, Marianne was unable to tell. He lived and moved as one in a dream surrounded by a world of dreams. His eyes were dull from looking into the dim distance of strange thoughts, and the smile which was rarely away from his lips was rather whimsically enduring than a sign of mirth.

But as he looked down at her from the buckboard, Marianne saw his expression clear to awareness of her. He even reached out and rested his hand on her head so that her face was tilted up to him.

"Honey," he said, "you're eating your heart out about something. How come?"

"Red Perris is overdue," she said. "But I don't want to bother you with my troubles, Dad."

"Red Perris? Who's he?"

"Don't you remember? I told you how he rode Rickety. And now I've sent for him to come and hunt Alcatraz—because once that man-killing horse is dead, it will be easy to get the mares back. And every day counts— every day the mares are getting wilder!"

"What mares?" Then he nodded. "I remember. And they ain't nothing but that worrying you, Marianne."

His expression of concern vanished; his glance wandered far east where the shades were already brimming the valleys.

"I'll be getting on, then, honey."

All at once, for pity at thought of him driving into the lonely silences, she caught his hand. It was still lean, hard of palm, sinewy with strength of which most extreme age, indeed, would never entirely rob it. And the touch of those strong fingers called back to her mind the picture of Oliver Jordan as he had been, a kingly man among men. Tears came into the eyes of Marianne.

"But where are you going?" she asked him gently. "And why do you never let me go with you, dear?"

"You?" he chuckled. "Waste time driving out nowheres with an old codger like me? I didn't give you all that schooling to have you throw your life away doing things like that. Don't you bother about me, Marianne. I'm just going to drift over yonder around Jackson Peak. You see?"

"But who is there, and what is there?"

He merely rubbed his knuckles across his forehead and then shook his head. "I dunno. Nothing much. It's tolerable quiet, though. And you get the smell of the pines the minute the trail starts climbing. Sort of a lazy place to go, but then I've turned into a lazy man, honey. Just sitting and thinking is about all I'm good for, or most like just the sitting without the thinking. Why, Marianne, where'd you get them tears?"

She choked them back.

"I wish—I wish—" she began.

"That's right," he nodded. "Keep right on wishing things. That's what I been doing lately. And wishing things is better than doing them. The way kids are, that's the best way to be. S'long, Marianne."

She stepped back, trying valiantly to smile, and he raised a cautioning finger, chuckling: "Look here, now, don't you go to bothering your head about me. Just save your worrying for this Perris gent."

He clucked to the greys and their sudden start threw him violently against the back of the seat.

The promise of that start, however, was by no means borne out by the pace into which they immediately fell, which was a dog-trot executed with trailing hoofs that raised little wisps of dust at every stride. She saw the lines slacken and hang loosely to every swing of the buckboard. Had she not, ten years before, trembled at the sight of this same team dashing into the road, high-headed, eyes of fire, and the reins humming with the strength of Oliver Jordan's pull?

The buckboard jolted slowly down the road and swung out of sight, but Marianne Jordan remained for long moments, staring after her father. Every time they passed through one of these interviews—and today's talk had been longer than most—she always felt that she had been pushed a little farther away from him. At the very time of his life when his daughter should have become a comfort to him, Oliver Jordan withdrew himself more and more from the world, and she could not but feel that his evening drives through the silences of the hill were dearer and closer to him than his daughter. The buckboard reappeared, lurching up a farther knoll, and then rolled out of sight to be seen no more. And Marianne felt again, what she had often felt before, seeing her father drive away in this fashion, that some day Oliver Jordan would never come back from the hills.

A moment later half a dozen of the cowpunchers came into view with the unmistakable form of Lew Hervey in the lead. He was a big-looking man in the saddle and he showed himself to the greatest advantage by riding rigidly erect with his head thrown a little back, so that the loose brim of his sombrero was continually in play about his face. For all her dislike of him she could not but admit that he was the beau ideal of the fine horseman. The dominant leader showed in every line and it was no wonder that the cowpunchers feared and respected him. Besides, there were many tales of his prowess with rifle and revolver to make him stand out in bolder relief.

She saw the riders disappear in the direction of the corrals and then turned back towards the house. Unquestionably it was to avoid sight of his men returning from their day's work that Oliver Jordan usually drove off at this time of the day; it brought home to him too keenly the many times when he himself had ridden back by the side of Lew Hervey from a day of galloping in the wind; it crushed him with a sense of the impotence into which his life had fallen. Indeed, unless some vital change came, her father must soon mourn himself into a grave. For the first time Marianne clearly perceived this. Oliver Jordan was wasting for grief over his lost freedom just as some youthful lover might decline because of the death of his mistress. The shock of this perception brought Marianne to a halt. When she looked up Shorty and Red Perris were not a hundred yards away, swinging along at a steady lope!

All sad thoughts were whisked from her mind as a gust whirls dead leaves away and shows the green grass beneath, newly growing. How it lifted her heart to see him. But she looked down, with a cold falling of gloom, at her blue gingham dress. That was not as she wished to appear. She could be in her riding costume, with the rather mannish blouse and loosely tied cravat, spurs on her boots and quirt in her hand as became the mistress and ruling force of a big ranch. Then she received sudden and convincing proof that mere outward appearances meant nothing in the life of Red Jim Perris. He took off his hat and swung it in greeting. There was a white flash of his teeth as he laughed, a red flash of his amazing hair in the sunset light. Then he was pulling up and swinging down to the ground. He came to meet her with his hat dangling in one hand and the other extended.

Typically Western, she thought, that in their second meeting he should act like an old friend. Delightfully Western, too! Under his straight-glancing eyes, his open smile of pleasure, new confidence came in Marianne, new self-reliance. The grip of his hand sent strength up her arm and into her heart.

"I'd given you up," she admitted.

"Mighty sorry it took so long," said Perris. "You see, I was right in the middle of a little poker game that hung on uncommon long. But when it finished up, me and Shorty come as fast as we could. Eh, Shorty?"

"Huh!" grunted Shorty. Marianne looked to her messenger for the first time.

He sat his saddle loosely, one hand falling heavily on the pommel, and his head bent. He did not raise it to meet her glance, but rolled his eyes up in a gloomy scowl which flitted over her face and then came to a rest on the face of Red Jim Perris. A frown of weariness puckered the brow of Shorty. Purple, bruised places of sleeplessness surrounded his eyes. And every line of age or worry or labor was graven more deeply on his face.

"Huh!" grunted Shorty again, mumbling his words very much like a drunkard. "I've killed my Mamie hoss, that's all!"

And with this gloomy retort, he urged the mare to a down-headed trot. In fact, the staunch little brown mare staggered on tired legs and her sides heaved like bellows. The grey horse of Red Jim Perris was in hardly better condition.

"I wanted you quickly," said Marianne, a little horrified. "But I didn't ask you to kill your horses coming."

"Kill 'em?" said Perris, and he cast a sharp glance of disapproval at her. "Not much! That hoss of mine is a pile fagged. I aim to get her that way. But she'll be fit as a fiddle in the morning. I ride her till she's through and never a step more. I know the minute she's through working on muscle and starts working on her nerve, and when that time comes, I stop. I've put up in the middle of nowheres to let her get back her wind. Kill her? Nope, lady, and the only reason Shorty's hoss was so used up was because he plumb insisted on keeping up with us!"

And Marianne nodded. Ordinarily such a speech would have drawn argument from her. Indeed, her own submissiveness startled her as she found herself gently inviting the fire eater to come into the house and learn in detail the work which lay before him.

CHAPTER XII
FROM THE HIP

SHORTY rode for the bunkhouse instead of the corrals and tumbling out of the saddle he staggered through the door. Inside, the cowpunchers sat about enjoying a before-dinner smoke and the coolness which the evening wash had brought to their wind-parched skins. Shorty reeled through the midst of them to his bunk and collapsed upon it.

Not a man stirred. Not an eye followed him. No matter what curiosity was burning in their vitals, etiquette demanded that they ask no questions. If in no other wise, the Indian has left his stamp on the country in the manners of the Western riders.

In the meantime, Shorty lay on his back with his arms flung out crosswise, his eyes closed, his breath expelled with a moan and drawn in with a rattle.

"Slim!" he called at length.

Slim raised his little freckled face which was supported by a neck of uncanny length, and he blinked unconcernedly at his bunkie. He and Shorty were inseparable companions.

"Take the saddle off my horse and put 'er up," groaned Shorty. "I'm dead beat!"

"Maybe you been chasing Perris on foot," observed Lew Hervey. Direct questions were still not in order, but often a man could be taunted into speech.

"Damn Perris and damn him black," retorted Shorty, opening his eyes with a snap and letting a glance blaze into space. "Of all the leather-skinned, mule-muscled, wrong-headed gents I ever seen he's the outlastingest."

"You sure got your vocabulary all warmed up," observed Little Joe, so-called because of two hundred pounds of iron-hard sinew and muscle. Slim was wandering towards the door to execute his mission, but he kept his head cocked towards his prostrated friend to learn as much as possible before he left. "Which I disremember," went on Little Joe thoughtfully, "of you ever putting so many words together without cussing. Perris must of give you some Bible study down to Glosterville."

It brought Shorty up on one bulging elbow and he glared at Little Joe.

"Bible?" snorted Shorty. "His idea of a Bible is fifty-two cards and a joker. He does his praying with one foot on a footrail."

"He'll sure fit in fine here," drawled Little Joe. "What with a girl for our boss and a hired hoss-catcher, none of us being good enough to take the job, we-all will get a mighty fine rep around these parts. You done yourself proud bringing him up here, Shorty."

"Laugh, damn you," said Shorty, heated to such a point that he half-forgot his exhaustion. "You ain't been through what I been through. You ain't man enough to of lasted." The imputation sobered Little Joe and he shrugged his massive shoulders significantly. Shorty's laugh was shrill with contempt. "Oh, you're big enough," he sneered. "But what does beef count agin a lightning flash?" He grew reminiscent. "I seen him bluff down the Wyoming Kid, yesterday."

A religious silence spread in the bunkhouse. The cowpunchers sat as stiff as though in Sunday store-clothes. Shorty took advantage of this favoring hush.

"I find him sitting in at a game of poker and I give him the girl's letter. He shakes it open saying: 'See that ten and raise you ten more.' I look over his shoulder as he flips up his cards. He's got a measly pair of deuces! Then he reads the letter and hands it back to me. 'Is it as bad as all that?' he says. 'See that other five and raise you twenty.' 'You're too strong for me Red,' says the gent that was bucking him—and lays down to that pair of deuces! I read the letter:

"'Dear Mr. Perris,

"'I know you don't like to hire out. But this is a job where you won't have a boss. The chestnut horse that nearly killed Manuel Cordova— Alcatraz—has come to my ranch and stolen half a dozen valuable mares. Will you come up and try to get rid of him for me? The job seems to be too big for my men. Name your own terms.

"'Cordially yours,

"'Marianne Jordan.'

"I hands him back the letter while he rakes in his winnings. 'I wouldn't go as far as she does about the men she's got,' I says, 'but the hoss is sure a fast thinking, fast moving devil.'

"'Well,' says he, 'it sort of sounds good to me. Soon as this game busts up we'll start. They's only four of us. Won't you take a hand?'

"Well, that game run on forty hours. Every time I got busted he staked me agin like a millionaire. But finally we was both flat.

"'All right,' says he, 'I got a purse light enough for travel now. Let's start.'

"'Without no sleep?' says I.

"'Have it your own way,' says he. 'We'll have a snooze and then start.'

"We didn't have the price of another room. He took me up to his room and makes me take the bed while he curls up on the floor. The next minute he's snoring while I was still arguing about not wanting to take the bed.

"Minute later I was asleep, but didn't seem my eyes were more'n close when he gives me a shake.

"'Five o'clock,' says he, 'and time to start.'

"We'd gone to bed about twelve but I wasn't going to let him put anything over on me. He bums a breakfast off the hotel, stalls 'em on his bill, and then we hit the road, him singing every step of the way and me near dead for sleep. I got so mad I couldn't talk. That damn singing sure was riding my nerves. I tried to take it out on a squirrel that run across the road but I missed him.

"'Tell you what, partner,' says Perris, 'for a quick shot, shooting from the hip is the only stuff.'

"'Shooting from the hip at squirrels?' says I. 'I've read about that sort of stuff in a book, but it never was done out of print.'

"'Just a matter of practice,' says he.

"'Huh,' says I, 'I'm here to see and do my talking afterwards.'

"Just then another squirrel pops across the trail dodging like a yearling trying to get back to the herd. Quick as a wink out comes Red's gun. It just does a flip out of the holster and bang! The dust jumped right under the squirrel's belly. Bang! goes the gat again and Mister Squirrel's tail is chopped plumb in two and then he ducks down his hole by the side of the trail and we hear him squealing and chattering cusswords at us.

"I never see such shooting in my life. But Perris puts up his gun and gets red as a girl when two gents ask her for the same dance.

"'I'm plumb out of practice,' he says. 'Anyways, I guess I been talking too much. You'll have to excuse me, Shorty!'

"And he meant it. He wasn't talking guff. Didn't seem possible anybody could shoot as fast and straight as that, but Perris was all cut up because he'd missed and he didn't do no more singing for about half an hour. And I needed that time for a lot of thinking. Made up my mind that if anybody wanted to make trouble for Perris they could count me out of the party.

"And he kept on singing, when he started again, all the way to the ranch and me wondering when I was going to go to sleep and fall off. I tried to make talk. Seen a queer looking fob he wore for his watch pocket. Asked him where he got it.

"'Tell you about it,' he says. 'Comes from me being plumb peaceable.' I remembered some of the things I'd heard about Red Perris in Glosterville and didn't say nothing. I just swallowed hard and took a squint at a cloud. 'Four or five years back,' he says, 'when they was more liquor and ambition floating around these parts, I was up in a little cross-roads saloon in Utah, near Gunterville. Saloon was pretty jammed with folks, all strangers to me. I wasn't packing a gun. Never do when I'm in a crowd, if I can help it. Well, I got into a little game of stud, and things were running pretty easy for me when a big gent across the table that had been losing hard and drinking hard ups and says he allows I sure have the cards talking. It sort of riled me. I tell him pretty liberal what I think of him and all like him. I go back into the past and give him a nice little description all about his ancestors. I aim to wind up with an invite to step outside and have it out with fists, but he don't wait. Right in the middle of my sermon he outs with a gat and blazes away at me. The slug drills me in the thigh and I go down.

"'Well, this is the slug. And I been wearing it to remind me that I particular want to meet up with that same gent before he gets too old for a gunfight!'"

Here Shorty paused and sighed, shaking his bullet-head. And a deep murmur of appreciation passed around the room. Shorty sank back again on the bunk and turned his broad back on the crowd.

"Don't nobody wake me for chuck," he warned them. "I've just finished cramming a month into four days and I got a night off coming."

Instantly his snoring began but it was some moments before anyone spoke. Then it was Little Joe in his solemn bass voice.

"Sounds man-sized," he declared. "Wears a bullet for a watch-fob, busts hosses for fun, sleeps one day a week, and don't work under a boss. Hervey, you'll have to put on kid gloves when you talk to that Perris, eh? Hey, where you going?"

"He's going out to think it over!" chuckled another. "He needs air, and I don't blame him. Just as soon be foreman over a wildcat as over a gent like Perris. There goes the gong!"

CHAPTER XIII
THE BARGAIN

BUT in spite of the dinner bell, Hervey made for the corrals instead of the house, roped and saddled the fastest pony in his string, jogged out to the eastern trail, and then sent his mount at a run into the evening haze. After a time he drew back to a more moderate gait, but still the narrow firs shot smoothly and swiftly past him for well over half an hour until the twilight settled into darkness and the treetops moved past the horseman against a sky alive with the brighter stars of the mountains. He reached the hills. The trail tangled into zigzag lines, tossing up and down, dodging here and there. And in one of these elbow turns, a team of horses loomed huge and black above him, and against the stars behind the hilltop it seemed as though the team were stepping out into the thin air. Behind them, Lew Hervey made out the low body of the buckboard and on the seat a squat, bunched figure with head dropped so low that the sombrero seemed to rest flat on the shoulders.

Hervey raised his hand with a shout of relief: "Hey, Jordan!"

The brakes crashed home, but the impetus of the downgrade bore the wagon to the bottom of the little slope before it came to a stop and Hervey was choked by the cloud of dust. He fanned a clear path for his voice.

"It's me. Hervey." And he came close to the wagon.

"Well, Lew?" queried the uninterested voice of the master.

Hervey leaned a little from the saddle and peered anxiously at the "big boss." He counted on creating a panic with his news. But a man past hope might very well be a man past fear. Hopeless Oliver Jordan certainly had been since his accident, hopeless and blind. That blindness had enabled Hervey to reap tidy sums out of his management of the ranch, and now that the coming of the sharp-eyed girl had cut off his sources of revenue he was ready to fight hard to put himself back in the saddle as unquestioned master of the Valley of the Eagles. But he could only work on Jordan through fear and what capacity for that emotion remained in the rancher. He struck at once.

"Jordan, have you got a gun with you?"

"Gun? Nope. What do I need a gun for?"

"Take this, then. It's my old gat. You know it pretty near as well as I do."

A nerveless hand accepted the heavy weapon and allowed it to sink idly upon his knee.

"How come?" drawled Jordan, and the heart of Lew Hervey sank. This was certainly not the voice of a man liable to panic.

"You and me got a bad time coming, Jordan, when we get to the ranch. He's there, and he's a devil for a fight!"

"Who?"

"Him! You remember that fight you got into in that saloon up in Wyoming? That night you and me was at the cross-roads saloon and you got off your feed with red-eye?"

The figure on the seat of the buckboard grew taller.

"Do I remember? Aye, and I'll never forget! The one downright bad thing I've ever done, Hervey. It was the infernal red-eye that made me a crazy man. You should of let me go back and see how bad he was hurt, Lew!"

"Nope. I was right. Best thing a gent can do after he's dropped his man is to climb a hoss and feed it leather."

"He didn't have a gun," groaned Jordan heavily. "But I forgot it. The red-eye got to working on me. I was losing. It was the one rotten yaller thing I ever done, Lew!"

"I know. And now he's here. He's Red Perris!"

"Red Perris!" breathed Oliver Jordan. "The man Marianne sent for? Why—why it's like fate, her bringing him right to the ranch!"

Hervey was discreetly silent.

"But," cried Jordan suddenly, and there was a ghost of the old ring in his voice, "I dropped him once by a crooked play and now I'll drop him fair and square, if he's here looking for trouble! I don't want your help, Lew. Mighty fine of you to offer it, but I ain't plumb forgot how to shoot. I don't want help!"

Hervey waited a moment for that heat of defiance to die away. Then he said with the quiet of certainty: "No use, Jordan. No use at all. Shorty seen this gent do some shooting on the way up to the ranch. He pulled on a squirrel that dodged across the trail. First slug knocked dust into the squirrel's belly-fur and the second chipped off his tail. Both of them slugs would have landed dead-center in a target as big as the body of a man!"

He paused again. He could hear the heavy breathing of Oliver Jordan and the figure of the driver swayed a little back and forth in the seat as a man will do when his mind is swinging from one alternative to another.

"He done that shooting from the hip," added Hervey, as though by afterthought.

There was a gasp from Jordan.

"Good God, Lew! You don't mean that!"

"That's what he done the shooting for—to show Shorty how to get off a quick shot. Shorty says he got his gun out and fired inside the time it'd take a common gun-man to wink twice. And that's why you and me have got to face him together, chief. You know I ain't particular yaller. But I'd as soon tackle a machine gun with a pea-shooter as run into this Perris all by myself. He's bad medicine, chief!"

"Two to one. That'd be worse'n murder, Lew. Neither you nor me could ever hold up a head around these parts again if the two of us jumped one gent."

"I know it," said Hervey solemnly. "But it's better to be shamed than to be dead. That's the way I figure. And I ain't so sure that both of us together could win out."

There was another interval of silence, far more important than many words. Through the hush Hervey, with a beating heart, strove to peer into the mind of the rancher.

"I'll go back and face him all by myself," said Jordan huskily. "I'll let him rub out that old score. If he finishes me—well, what good am I in the world, anyway? No good, Lew. I'm done for just as much as though somebody had plugged me with a gat. Let Perris finish the job." He added hastily: "But these five years have changed me a lot. Maybe he won't know me."

"You ain't changed that much, Jordan. Look at Howlands. He hadn't seen you for eight years. He knew you right off."

"Ay," growled Jordan. "That's true enough. But what makes you so sure that Perris is so hot after me. Ain't there been time enough for him to cool down?"

With the skill of a connoisseur, saving his choicest morsel for the end, Hervey had waited for the most favorable opportunity before striking home with his most convincing item.

"You remember you drilled him in the leg, chief?"

"I remember everything. The whole damned affair has never been out of my head for a whole day. I've gone over every detail of it a thousand times, Lew!"

"So has Perris," answered Lew Hervey solemnly. "That slug of yours—when the doctor cut it out of his leg he had it fixed up and now he wears it for a fob so's he won't forget the gent that shot him down that night when he wasn't armed!"

"Most like that's why he's practiced so much with a gun," muttered Jordan. "He's been getting ready for me."

"Most like," said the gloomy Hervey, but his voice well-nigh trembled with gratification.

The head of Jordan bowed again, but this time, as Hervey shrewdly guessed, it was in thought, not in despair.

"Why," chuckled Jordan at last, "what we wasting all this fool time about? You just slip back to the ranch and fire Perris."

In the favoring dark, Hervey threw back his head and made a grimace of joy. Exactly as he had prefigured, this talk was going. Every card was being played into his hand as though his wishes were subconsciously entering and ruling the mind of the chief.

"I can't do it," he answered firmly.

"You can't? Ain't you foreman?"

"No," said Hervey, and a trace of bitterness came into his voice. "I used to be. But you know as well as me that I'm only a straw boss now. Miss Marianne is running things, big and small. Besides, she picked up Perris. And she won't let him go easy, I tell you!"

"What do you mean by that, Hervey?"

"I seen her face when she met him. I was standing outside the bunkhouse. And she sure was tolerable pleased to see him."

A tremendous oath burst from Jordan.

"You mean she's sweet on this—this Perris?" But he added: "Why should that rile me? Maybe he's all right."

"He's one of them flashy dressers," said Lew Hervey. "Silk shirts and swell bandannas and he wears shopmade boots and keep 'em all shined up. Besides, it's dead easy for him to talk to a girl. He's the kind that get on with 'em pretty well."

The innuendo brought a huge roar from Oliver Jordan.

"By God, Lew, d'you think that's what it means? I thought she talked pretty strong about this Perris!"

"Maybe I've said too much," said Hervey.

"Not a word too much," said Jordan heartily, and reaching through the night he found the hand of Hervey and wrung it heartily. "I know how square you are, Lew. I know how you've stood by me. I'd stake my last dollar on you!"

Hervey blessed again the mercy of the darkness which concealed the crimson that spread hotly over his face. There was enough truth in what the rancher said to make the untruths the more painful. Before the accident Hervey had, indeed, been all that anyone could ask in a manager. But when too much authority came into his hands owing to the crippling of his chief, the temptation proved too strong for resistance. It was all so easy. A few score of cows run off here and there were never noted, and his share in the profit was fifty-fifty. Indeed, as the hand of Jordan crushed over his own he came perilously near to making a clean breast of everything, but the memory of his fat and growing bank-account gagged the confession.

"If that's the way things are standing," Jordan was saying, "we got to get rid of this skunk Perris. Good-looking, as I remember him, and Marianne is so darned lonely on the ranch that she might begin to take him serious and— Hervey, I'll give you a written note. That'll be authority. I'll give you a note to Marianne, telling her that I've got to go across the mountains and that I want you to have the running of the place till I get back. I guess that'll give you a free hand, Lew! You fire that Perris, and when he's gone, send me word over to the hotel in Lawrence. That's where I'll go."

Hervey appeared dubious with great skill.

"I'll take the note, Jordan," he said, putting all the despair he could summon into his tone. "But it sure goes hard—the idea of losing my place up here. I've been in the Valley so long, you see, that it's like a home to me."

"And who the devil said anything about you leaving? Ain't I just now about to give you a note to run the ranch while I'm gone?"

"Sure you are. And I'll take it—and fire Perris. But when you come back— that's the end of me!"

"What?"

"You know how your daughter is. She'll plumb hate me when I come back with orders to run things. She'll think I asked for 'em."

"I'll tell her different."

"Were you ever able to convince her, once she made up her mind?"

"H-m-m," growled Jordan.

"And she'll never rest till things are so hot for me that I got to get out. Not that I grudge it, Jordan. I'd give up more than this job for your sake. Only it sure makes me homesick to think about starting out at my time of life and riding herd for a strange outfit."

"You ride for another outfit?" said Jordan. "And after you've worked this game on Perris for me? I'll tell you what, Lew, if you get Perris safe off the ranch you can stop worrying. You're foreman for life! You have my word for it."

"But suppose—" protested Hervey faintly.

"Suppose nothing. You have my word. Besides, I'm tired of talking!"

With well-acted diffidence, Lew held out the paper, which Oliver Jordan snatched and smoothed on his knee. Then Hervey rode closer, lighted a match, and held it so that the rancher could see to write.

"Dear Marianne," scrawled the pencil, "this is to let you know that I have to go on business to—"

"Better not tell her where," suggested Hervey. "She might send after and ask a lot of bothersome questions. You know the way a woman is."

"You sure got a fine head for business, Lew," nodded Jordan, and continued his note: "to a town across the mountains and it may be a few days before I get back. I met Lew on the road, so I'm letting him take this note back to you Another thing: I've told Lew about several things I want done while I'm gone. Easier than explaining them all to you, honey, he can do them himself and tell you later.

Affectionately,"

As he scrawled the signature Hervey suggested softly: "Suppose you put down at the bottom: 'This will serve as authority to Lew Hervey to act in my name while I'm away.'"

"Sure," nodded Jordan, as he scribbled the dictated words. "Marianne is a stickler for form. She'll want something like that to convince her."

He shoved the paper into the trembling hand of Lew Hervey, and sighed with weariness.

"Chief," muttered Hervey, finding that even in the darkness he could not look into the tired, pain-worn face of the rancher, "I sure hope you never have no call to be sorry for this."

"Sorry? I ain't bothering about that. So long, Lew."

But Lew Hervey had suddenly lost his voice. He could only wave his adieu.

CHAPTER XIV
STRATEGY

NEVER had Red Perris passed a night of such pleasant dreams. For never, indeed, had he been so exquisitely flattered as during the preceding evening when Marianne Jordan kept him after dinner in the ranchhouse while the other hired men, as was their custom, loitered to smoke their after-dinner cigarettes in the moist coolness of the patio. For the building was on the Spanish-Mexican style. The walls were heavy enough to defy the most biting cold of winter and the most searching sun in summer. And they marched in a wide circle around an interior court which was bordered with a clumsy arcade of 'dobe pillars. By daylight the defects in construction were rather too apparent. But at night the effect was imposing, almost grand.

But while the cowhands smoked in the patio, the noise of their laughter and their heavy voices penetrated no louder than the dim humming of bees to the ear of Red Jim Perris, sitting tête-à-tête with Marianne in an inner room. And he did not envy the sprawling freedom of those outside.

Pretty girls had come his way now and again during his wanderings north and south and east and west through the mountain deserts. But never before had he seen one in such a background. She had had the good taste to make the inside of the house well-nigh as Spanish as its exterior. There were cool, dim spaces in the big rooms; and here and there were bright spots of color. Her very costume for the evening showed the same discrimination. She wore drab riding clothes. But from her own garden she had chosen a scentless blossom of a kind which Red Perris had never seen before. The absent charm of perfume was turned into a deeper coloring, a crimson intense as fire in the darkness of her hair. That one touch of color, and no more, but it gave wonderful warmth to her eyes and to her smile.

And indeed she was not sparing in her smiles. Red Jim Perris pleased her, and she was not afraid to show it. To be sure, she talked of the business before them, but she talked of it only in scattered phrases. Other topics drew her away. A score of little side-issues carried her away. And Jim Perris was glad of the diversions.

For the only thing which he disliked in her, the only thing which repelled him time and again, was this eagerness of hers to have the chestnut stallion killed. She spoke of Alcatraz with a consuming hatred. And Perris was a little horrified. He knew that Alcatraz had stolen away the six mares, and Marianne explained briefly and eloquently how much the return of those mares meant to her self-respect and to the financial soundness of the ranch. But this, after all, was a small excuse for an ugly passion. If he could have known that with her own eyes she had seen the chestnut crush Cordova to shapelessness and almost to death, the mystery might have been cleared. But Marianne could not refer to that terrible memory. All she could say was that Alcatraz must be killed—at once! And she said it with her eyes on fire with detestation.

Indeed, that touch of angry passion in her was the flower of Hermes to Red

Jim, keeping him from complete infatuation when she sang to him, playing her own lightly-touched accompaniment at the piano. He had never been entertained like this before. And when a girl sang a love ballad and at the same time looked at him with eyes at once serious and laughing, he had to set his teeth and shake himself to keep from taking the words of the poet too literally. Perhaps Marianne was going a little farther than she intended. But after all, every good woman has a tremendous desire to make men happy, and handsome Jim Perris with his straight, steady eyes and his free laughter was such a pleasant fellow to work with that Marianne quite forgot moderation.

And before the evening was over, Jim had come within a hair's breadth of plunging over the cliff and confessing his admiration in terms so outright that Marianne would have closed up her charming gaiety as a flower closes up its beauty and fragrance at the first warning chill of night. A dozen times Red Perris came to this alarming point, but he was always saved by remembering that this delightful girl had brought him here for the purpose of—killing a horse. And that memory chilled Jim to the very core of his manly heart.

Of course he knew that wild-running stallions who steal saddle stock must be cleared from a range, and by shooting if necessary. He would have received such an order from a man and never thought the less of him, but the command was too stern for the smiling lips of Marianne. To be sure, Perris was by no means a gentle rider. In fact, he rode so *very* hard that only fine horses could measure up to his demands, and who, since the world began, has ridden many fine horses without coming to love the entire race? Red Perris, at least, was such a man, and indeed he spent many an hour dreaming of some happy day when he should find beneath him a mount with speed like an eagle, soul of a lion, and the gentle, trusting heart of a child.

Finally, the evening ended. He left the house and the puzzled smile of Marianne behind him and went to the bunkhouse and a sleep of happy dreams. But every dream ended with the thought of a wild chestnut running into the circle of his rifle's sights, leaping into the air at the report of his gun, and dropping inert on the grass. What wonder, then, that when he wakened he thought of Marianne Jordan with mixed emotions? Perhaps the really important point was that he thought of her so much, whether for good or evil.

He went in with the other men to breakfast in the long dining-room of the ranch house, and there was Marianne Jordan again presiding at the head of the table. But half of the glamour of the evening before was gone from her and she kept her eyes seriously lowered, frowning. In fact, she had much to think about, for late the preceding evening Lew Hervey had come to her and showed her the first note that her father had written. She was not alarmed by this sudden trip over the mountains. There had been so many vagaries in the actions of Oliver Jordan in the past few months that this unannounced drive to an undetermined destination was not particularly surprising. It was only the delegation of such authority to Hervey that astonished her.

She forgot even Red Jim Perris and the lost Coles horses in her abstraction, for whenever she looked down the table she saw nothing saving the erect, burly form of the foreman, swelling, so it seemed to her, with a newly acquired and aggressive importance. However, he had the written word of her father, and she had to set her teeth over her irritation and digest it as well as he could.

Hervey had presented reasonable excuses, to be sure. There was certain work of fence-repairing, certain construction of sheds which he had called to the attention of Oliver Jordan and which Jordan had commissioned him to overlook during his absence.

"I told him they wasn't any use in writing out a note like this one," Hervey had assured her, "but you know how the chief is, these days. Sort of set in his ways when he makes up his mind about anything."

And this was so entirely true that she was half-inclined to dismiss the whole matter from her mind. Oliver Jordan paid so little heed to the running of the ranch and when he did make a suggestion he was so peremptory about it, that this commission to Hervey was not altogether astonishing. Nevertheless, it kept her absent-minded throughout breakfast.

Red Perris was naturally somewhat offended by the blankness of her eye as she passed him over. She had been so extremely intimate and cordial the night before that this neglect was almost an insult. Perhaps she had only been playing a game—trying to amuse herself during a dull hour instead of truly wishing to please him. He grew childishly sulky at the thought. After all, there *was* a good deal of the spoiled child about Red Jim. He had had his way in the world so much that opposition or neglect threw him into a temper.

And he stamped out of the dining-room ahead of the rest of the men, his head down, his brows black. Lew Hervey, following with the other men, had noted everything. It behooved him to be on the watch during the time of trial and triumph and at breakfast he had observed Red Perris looking at the girl a dozen times with an anticipatory smile which changed straightway to glumness when her glance passed him carelessly by. And now Hervey communicated his opinions to the others on the way to the bunkhouse to get their things for the day's riding.

"Our new friend, the gun-fighter," he said, pointedly emphasizing the last phrase, "ain't none too happy this morning. Marianne give him a smile last night and he was waiting for another this morning. He sure looks cut up, eh?"

The bowed head and rounded shoulders of Red Perris brought a chuckle from the cowpunchers. They were not at all kindly disposed towards him. Too much reputation is a bad thing for a man to have on his hands in the West. He is apt to be expected to live up to it every moment of his waking hours. Not a man in the Valley of the Eagles outfit but was waiting to see the newcomer make the first move towards bullying one of them. And such a move they were prepared to resent en masse. That Marianne might have made a good deal of a fool out of Perris, as Hervey suggested, pleased them immensely.

"Maybe the ranch suits him pretty well," suggested Slim, ironically. "Maybe he figures it might be worth his while to pick it up by marrying the old man's girl. Eh, Lew?"

Lew Hervey shrugged his shoulders. He did not wish to directly accuse the gun-fighter of anything, for talk is easily traced to its source and the account of Shorty had filled the foreman with immense respect for the fighting qualities of Red Perris. However, he was equally determined to rouse a hostile sentiment towards him among the cowhands.

"Well," said Lew, "you can't blame a gent for playing for high stakes if he's going to gamble at all. I guess Red Perris is all right. A kid like him can't help being a little proud of himself."

"Damn fat-head," growled Slim, less merciful, "sat right next to me and didn't say two words all through breakfast. Ain't going to waste no words on common cowpunchers, maybe."

So the first impression of Red Jim was created on the ranch, an impression which might be dispelled by the first real test of the man, or which in the absence of such a test might cling to him forever: Perris was a conceited gun-fighter, heart-breaker, and bully. The men who trooped into the bunkhouse behind him already hated him with a religious intensity; in ten minutes, they might have accepted him as a bunkie! For your true Western cowpuncher, when all is said and done, unites with Spartan stoicism a Spartan keenness of suspicion.

It was not hard for the foreman to see the trend of events. Something had roused an ugly mood in Perris. It might be, as he surmised, the girl. No matter what, he was obviously not in a mood to bear tampering with. Hervey determined to force the issue at once, knowing that his other men would be a solid unit behind him.

"Hey there, Red!" he called, cheerily enough, but brusquely, and then, bending over to fuss at a spur, he winked broadly at the other men. They were instantly keen for the baiting of Perris, whatever form it might take.

"Well?" said Red Perris.

"Trot over to the corral and rope that Roman-nosed buckskin with the white stockings on her forelegs, will you? I got a few things to tend to in here."

Now there was nothing entirely unheard of in a foreman ordering one of his men to catch a saddle horse for him. But usually such things were done by request rather than demand, and moreover, there was something so breezy in the manner of Hervey, taking the compliance of Red so for granted, that the latter raised his head slowly and turned to the foreman with a gloomy eye. He had come to the ranch to hunt a wild horse, not to play valet to a foreman.

"Partner," drawled Red Perris, and the silken smoothness of his tones was ample proof that he was enraged. "I don't know the ways you folks have up here, but around the parts where I've been, a gent that's big enough to ride is big enough to saddle his own hoss."

The reply of Lew Hervey was just sharp enough to goad the newcomer—just soft enough to stay on the windward side of an insult.

"I'll tell you," he said quietly. "Around the Valley of the Eagles, the boys do what the foreman asks 'em to do, most generally. And the foreman don't play favorites. I'm waiting for that hoss, Perris."

Perris rolled a cigarette, and smiled as he looked at Hervey. It was a sickly smile, his lips being white and stiff. And in another, it might have been considered a sign of fear. In Red Perris everyone there knew it was simply the badge of a rising fury. They knew, by the same token, that he was as dangerous as he had been advertised. Men whom anger reddens are blinded by it; but those who turn pale never stop thinking. Meantime, Red Jim looked at Hervey and looked at the cowpunchers behind Hervey. It was not hard to see that in a pinch they would be solid behind their foreman. They watched him with a wolfish eagerness. Why they should be so instantly hostile he could not guess but he was enough of a traveller to be prepared for strange customs in strange places. There was only one important point: he would not saddle the buckskin. Moreover, at sight of their solid front and their aggressive sneers he grew fighting hot.

"How gents come in these parts," he said with deliberate scorn, "I dunno. And I don't care a damn. If they brush their foreman's boots and saddle his hosses for him, they can go ahead and do it. But I come up here to catch a wild hoss that the gents in the Valley of the Eagles couldn't get. That's my job, and nothing else."

The growl of his cowpunchers was sweetest music to the ear of Lew Hervey. He glanced at them as much as to say: "You see what I got on my hands?" Then he stepped forward and cleared his throat.

"You're young, kid," he declared. "When you grow up you'll know better'n to talk like this. But cowpunchers we ain't going to make no trouble for you. But I'll tell you short, Perris, you'll go out and rope that hoss or else roll your blankets and clear out. Understand? I was joking when I asked you to rope the hoss first. I wanted to see what sort were. Well, I see, and I don't like what I see."

"Hervey," began Perris, trembling with his passion "Hervey—"

"Wait a minute," said the foreman, "I know your kind. You sign your name with bullets. You pay your way with lead. You bully a crowd by fingering a gun-butt. Well, son, that sort of thing don't go in the Valley of the Eagles. Lay a hand on that gun and I'll have the boys tie you in knots and roll you in a barrel of tar we got handy. Perris, get that hoss for me, or get out!"

Red Perris sat down on the edge of his bunk. He made no move towards his revolver. Indeed, it lay almost arm's length away. Almost—everyone noted that. He crossed his legs and his glance wandered slowly up and down the line of grim faces.

"Partner," he said softly to Hervey, "I'm not going to get the hoss and I'm not going to get out. The next move is up to you. Is it tar?"

For a moment Hervey was dazed. No one could have foreseen such daredeviltry as this. At the same time, he was badly cornered. If his men rushed Red Perris, Red Perris would get his gun. And if Red Perris got his gun the first shot would be for Hervey.

"Hold on, boys," he called suddenly, above the angry curses of his men, "I'm not going to risk one of you in getting this fool. Miss Jordan hired him. She can fire him if I can't. Which we'll find out pronto. Slim, go get her, will you?"

Slim jumped through the door. They heard his footsteps fade away at a run.

And then, after an interval of steady silence, his voice began in the distance, replying to sharp, hurried inquiries of Marianne. In another moment Marianne was in the bunkhouse. Her glance shot from Hervey to Perris and back again.

"I knew you'd be up to something like this!" she cried. "I knew it, Lew Hervey!"

Hervey made a gesture of surrender.

"Ask the boys," he pleaded. "Ask them if I didn't try to go easy with him. But he's all teeth. He wants to bite. And we ain't going to put up with that sort of a gent here, I guess! I've ordered him off the ranch. Does that go with you?"

"Oh, Jim Perris," cried the girl. "*Why* have you let this happen!"

"I'm sure sorry," said Perris. He disdained further explanation.

"But," said Marianne, "I've got to have that terrible stallion killed. And who can do it but Jim Perris, Mr. Hervey?"

"Gimme time," said Lew, "and I'll do it."

She stamped her foot in anger.

"How you wheedled the authority out of my father, I don't know," she said. "But you have it and you can discharge him if you want. But he'll hear another side to this when he returns, Mr. Hervey, I promise you that!" She whirled on Red Jim. "Mr. Perris, if Mr. Hervey allows you to stay, will you remain for—a week, say, and try to get rid of Alcatraz for me? Mr. Hervey, will you let me have Mr. Perris for one week?"

There was more angry demand than appeal in her voice, but Hervey knew he must give way. After all, the way to carry this thing through was to use the high hand as little as possible. Oliver Jordan would certainly wait a week before he returned.

"I sure want to be reasonable, Miss Jordan," he said. "I'm only acting in your father's interests. Of course he can stay for a week."

She whirled away from him with a glance of angry suspicion which softened instantly as she faced Red Jim.

"You *will* stay?" she pleaded.

Sullen pride drew Jim one way; the bright, eager eyes drew him another.

"As long as you want," he said gravely.

CHAPTER XV
THE KING

If men may to some degree be classed in categories of bird and beast, one like the eagle, another like the bear, some swinish, some elephantine, some boldly leonine, unquestionably Red Perris must be likened to the cat tribe. To some the comparison would have seemed most opportune, having seen him in restless action; but the same idea might have come to one who saw him lying prone on a certain hilltop in the western foothills of the Eagle mountains, unmoving hour by hour, his rifle shoved out before him among the dead grasses, his chin resting on the back of his folded hands, and always his attentive eyes roved from point to point over the landscape below him. A cat lies passive in this manner half a day, watching the gopher hole.

It was not the first or the second time he had spent the afternoon in this place. For nearly a week he had given the better part of every day to the vigil on this hilltop. All this for very good reasons. During ten days after his first coming to the ranch he tried the ordinary methods of hunting down wild horses, and with a carefully posted string of half a dozen horses, he twice attempted to run down the outlaw, but he had never come within more than the most distant and hazardous rifle range. To be sure he had fired some dozen shots during the pursuits but they had been random efforts at times when the red chestnut was flashing off in the distance, fairly walking away from the best mounts the hunter could procure. Having logically determined that it was not in the power of horse flesh burdened with the weight of a rider to come within striking distance of the stallion, Red Jim Perris passed from action to quiescence. If he could not outrun Alcatraz he would outwait him.

First he studied the habits of the new king of the Eagle Mountains, day by day following the trail. It was not hard to distinguish after he had once measured the mighty stride of Alcatraz in full gallop and he came to know to a hair's breath the distances which the chestnut stepped when he walked or trotted or loped or galloped or ran. More than that, he could tell by the print of the four hoofs, all of the same size, the same roundness—token so dear to the heart of a horseman! By such signs he identified old and new trails until he could guess the future by the past, until he could begin to read the character of the stallion. He knew, for instance, the insatiable curiosity with which the chestnut studied his wilderness and its inhabitants. He had seen the trail looping around the spot where the rattler's length had been coiled in the sand, or where a tentative hoof had opened the squirrel's hole. On a night of brilliant moonshine, he had watched through his glass while Alcatraz galloped madly, tossing head and tail, and neighing at a low-swooping owl.

Great, foolish impulses came to Alcatraz; he might gather his mares about him and lead them for ten miles at a terrific pace and with a blind destination; he might leave them and scout far and wide, alone, always at dizzy speed. As the hunter stayed longer by his puzzling task, he began to wonder if this sprang from mere running instinct, or knowledge that he must keep himself in the pink of condition. Like a man, the preferences of Alcatraz were distinctly formed and well expressed. He disliked the middle day and during this period sought a combination of wind and shade. Only in the morning and in the evening he ranged for pasture or for pleasure. Impulse still guided him. Now and again he wandered to the eastern or the western mountains, then far into the hot heart of the desert, then, with incredible boldness, he doubled back to the well-watered lands of the Jordan ranch, leaped a fence, followed by the mares to whom he had taught the art of jumping, and fed fat under the very eye of his enemies.

The boldness of these proceedings taught Perris what he already knew, that the stallion knew man and hated as much as he dreaded his former masters. These excursions were temptings of Providence, games of hazard. Perris, gambler by instinct himself, understood and appreciated, at the same time that his anger at being so constantly outwitted, outdistanced, grew hot. Then there remained no kindness, only desire to make the kill. His dreams had come to turn on one picture—Alcatraz cantering in range of the waiting rifle!

That dream haunted even his walking moments as he lay here on the hilltop, wondering if he had not been mistaken in selecting this place of all the range. Yet he had chosen it with care as one of the points of passage for Alcatraz during the stallion's wanderings to the four quarters of his domains and though since he took up his station here an imp of the perverse kept the stallion far away, the watcher remained on guard, baked and scorched by the midday sun, constantly surveying the lower hills nearby or sweeping more distant reaches with his glass. This day he felt the long vigil to be definitely a failure, for the sun was behind the western summits and the time of deepening shadows most unfavorable to marksmanship had come. He swung the glass for the last time to the south; it caught the glint of some moving creature.

He focused his attention, but the object disappeared. A full five minutes passed before it came out of the intervening valley but then, bursting over the hilltop, it swept enormous into the power of the glass—Alcatraz, and at full gallop!

There was no shadow of a doubt, for though it was the first time he had been able to watch the stallion at close hand he recognized the long and effortless swing of that gallop. Next he remembered those stories of the charmed life and the tales he had mocked at before now became possible truths. He caught up his gun to make sure, but when his left hand slipped under the barrel to the balance and the butt of the gun pulled into the hollow of his shoulder, he became of rocklike steadiness. Swinging the gun to the left he caught Alcatraz full in the readly circle of the sights and over his set teeth the lips curled in a smile; the trail had ended! The slightest movement of his finger would beckon the life out of that marauder, but as one who tastes the wine slowly, inhales its bouquet, places the vintage, even so Red Perris delayed to taste the fruition of his work. Pivoted on his left elbow, he swung the rifle with frictionless ease and kept the galloping stallion steadily in the center of the sight.

He smiled grimly now at those fables of the charmed life and drew a bead just over the heart. The chestnut was very near. Along the glorious slope of his shoulder Perris saw the long muscles playing with every stride, and what strides they were! He floated rather than galloped; his hoofs barely flicked the ground, and it seemed to Jim Perris a shameful thing to smash that mechanism. He did not love horses; he was raised in a land where they were too strictly articles of use. But even as a machine he saw in Alcatraz perfection.

Not the body, then. He would drive the bullet home into the brain, the cunning brain which had conceived and executed all the mischief the chestnut had worked. Along the shining neck, so imperiously arched, Perris swung the sights and rested his head, at last, just below the ears with the forelock blown back between them by the wind of running. Slowly his finger closed on the trigger. It seemed that in the silence Alcatraz had found a signal of danger for now he swung that imperious head about and looked full at Red Perris. By his own act he had changed the aim of the hunter to a yet more fatal target—the forehead.

The heart of Perris leaped even as it had stirred, more than once, when he had looked into the eyes of fighting men. Here was an equal pride, an equal fierceness looking forth at him. Then he remembered the six mares somewhere at the center of the guarding circle which Alcatraz now drew. What a dauntless courage was here in the brute mind which, knowing the power of man, dared to rob him, to defy him! Truly this was the king of horses meant for higher ends than to serve as target of a Winchester. Ay, he could make his owner a king among men. Mounted on the back of the chestnut no enemy could overtake him; from that winged speed none could escape. The back of Alcatraz might be a throne! He could end all that boundless strength by one pressure of his finger but was that indeed a true conquest? It was calling to his aid a trick, it was using an unfair advantage, it seemed to Perris; but suppose that he, the rider who had never yet failed in the saddle, were to sit on the stallion—there would be a battle for the Gods to witness!

It was madness, sheer madness; it was throwing away the labor of the patient days of waiting and working; but to Perris it seemed the only thing to do. He leaped to his feet and brandished the gleaming rifle.

"Go it, boy!" he shouted. "We'll meet again!"

One snort from Alcatraz—then he changed to a red streak flashing down the hollow.

Before the stallion was out of sight, a cry rang down the wind. It was chopped off by the crack of a rifle, and Lew Hervey spurred from behind a neighboring hill and plunged after Alcatraz pumping shot on shot at the fugitive. In a frenzy Perris jerked his own gun to the shoulder and drew down on the pursuer, but the red anger cleared from his mind as he caught the burly shoulders of Hervey in the sights. He lowered the rifle with a grim feeling that he had never before been so close to a murder.

A moment later he began to chuckle behind his set teeth. No wonder they credited the chestnut with a charmed life. As he raced away gaining a yard at every leap, he swerved like a jackrabbit from side to side. Perhaps the deadly hum of bullets on many another chase had taught him this trick of dodging, but beyond all doubt when Hervey returned to the ranch that night he would have a tale of mystery. To preserve his self-respect as a good marksman, what else could he do?

In the meantime pursued and pursuer scurried out of sight beyond a hill; the gun barked far away and the echoes murmured lightly from the hollows. Then Perris turned his back and trudged homewards.

CHAPTER XVI
RED PERRIS: ADVOCATE

HE did not choose to live in the ranch because of Hervey and because it was too far removed from the scene of action. Instead, he selected a shack stumbling with age on the west slope of the Eagle Mountains. From his door many a time, with his glass, he picked out the shining form of Alcatraz and the mares in the distance; he had even been able to follow the maneuvers of the outlaw on several occasions when Hervey and his men pursued with relays of horses, and on the whole he felt that the site was such a position as a good general must prefer, being behind the lines but with a view which enabled him to survey the whole action. His quarters consisted of a single room while a shed leaned against the back wall with one space for a horse, the other portion of the shed being used as a mow for hay and grain.

It was the beginning of the long, still time of the mountain twilight when Red Perris climbed to the clearing in which the cabin stood. Ordinarily he would have set about preparing supper before the coming of the dark, but now he watered and saddled his cowpony, a durable little buckskin, and with a touch of the spurs sent him at a pitching gallop down the slope.

It was not a kindly thing to do but Red Perris was not a kindly man with horses and though he knew that it is hard on the shoulders of even a mustang to be ridden downhill rapidly, he kept on with unabated speed until he broke onto the well-established trail which led to the Jordan house. Then a second touch of the spurs brought the pony close to a full gallop. In fact, Perris was riding against time, for he guessed that Lew Hervey, after quitting the trail of Alcatraz, would veer straight towards the home place and there lay before Marianne an account of how the chosen hunter had allowed the stallion to slip through his hands. This, together with the fact that his week was up was enough to bring about his discharge, for he had seen sufficient of the girl to guess her fiery temper and he knew that she must have been harshly tried during the last weeks by his lack of success and by the continual sneers and mockery which the foreman and his followers had directed at the imported horse-catcher. Before sunset of that day he would have welcomed his discharge; now it loomed before him as the greatest of all possible catastrophes.

Soon he was swinging down an easy road with the tilled lands on one side, the pastures and broad ranges on the other, and even in the dim light he guessed the wealth which the estate was capable of producing. Even the deliberate mismanagement of Hervey was barely able to create a deficit and Perris grew hot when he thought of the foreman. His own dislikes found swift expression and were as swiftly forgotten; that a grown ranchman could nourish resentment towards a girl, and that because she was attempting to take charge of her own property, was well beyond his comprehension. For he had that quality which is common to all born leaders: he understood in what good and faithful service should consist; with this addition, that he was far more fitted to command than to be commanded.

It may be seen that there was a background of gloomy thought in his mind, yet from time to time he startled the mustang to a harder pace by a ringing burst of song. Remembering the windlike gallop of Alcatraz, it seemed to him that the buckskin was hardly keeping to a lope—as a matter of fact the cow pony was being ridden to the verge of exhaustion. So the songs of Perris kept the rhythm of the departed hoofs of wild Alcatraz and the shining form of the stallion wavered and danced in his mind.

The ranch building grew out of the dun evening and he smiled at the sight. The bank roll of Marianne had not been thick enough to enable her to do the reconstruction she desired, but at least she had been able to hire a corps of painters, so that the drab, weathered frame structures had been lifted into crimson and green roofs, white yellow, and flaming orange walls. "A little color is a dangerous thing," Marianne had said, somewhat overwisely, "but a great deal of it is pretty certain to be pleasing." So she had let her fancy run amuck, so to speak, and behind the merciful screen of trees there was now what Lew Hervey profanely termed: "A whole damn rainbow gone plumb crazy." Even Marianne at times had her doubts, but from a distance and by dint of squinting, she was usually able to reduce the conglomerate to a tolerably harmonious whole. "It's a promise of changes to come," she told herself. "It's a milestone pointing towards new goals." But the milestone set Perris chuckling. Yonder a scarlet roof burned through the shadows above moonwhite walls—that was a winter-shed for cows. Straight before him were the hot orange sides of the house itself. He dismounted at the arched entrance and walked into the patio.

The first thing that Perris heard was the most provocative and sneering tone of the foreman, and cursing the slowness of the buckskin, he realized that he had been beaten to his goal. He paused in the shadow of the arch to take stock of his position. The squat arcade of 'dobe surrounding the patio was lighted vaguely by a single lantern at his left. It barely served to make the shadowy outlines of the house visible, the heavy arches, roughly sketched doorways, and hinted at the forms of the cowpunchers who were ranged under the far arcade for their after-dinner smoke, all eagerly listening to the dialogue between the mistress and the foreman. When a breath of wind made the flame jump in the lantern chimney a row of grinning faces stood out from the shadow.

Marianne sat in a deep chair which made her appear girlishly slight. The glow of the reading lamp on the table beside her fell on her hair, cast a highlight on her cheek, and showed her hand lying on the open book in her lap, palm up. There was something about that hand which spoke to Perris of helpless surrender, something more in the gloomy eyes which looked up to the foreman where he leaned against a pillar. The voice drawled calmly to an end: "And that's what he is, this gent you got to finish what me and the rest started. Here he is to tell you that I've spoke the truth."

With the uncanny Western keenness of vision, Hervey had caught sight of the approaching Perris from the corner of his eye. He turned now and welcomed the hunter with a wave of his hand. Marianne drew herself up with her hands clasped together in her lap and though in this new attitude her face was in complete shadow, Perris felt her eyes burning out at him. His dismissal was at hand, he knew, and then the carelessly defiant speech which was forming in his throat died away. Sick at heart, he realized that he must cringe under the hand which was about to strike and be humble under the very eye of Hervey. He was no longer free and the chain which held him was the conviction that he could never be happy until he had met and conquered wild Alcatraz, that he was as incomplete as a holster without a gun or a saddle without stirrups until the speed and the great heart of the stallion were his to control and command.

"I've heard everything from Lew Hervey," said the girl, in that low strained voice which a woman uses when her self-control is barely as great as her anger, "and I suppose I don't need to say that after these days of waiting, Mr. Perris, I'm disappointed. I shall need you no longer. You are free to go without giving notice. The experiment has been—unfortunate."

He felt that she had searched as carefully as her passion permitted to find a word that would sting him. The hot retort leaped to his lips but he closed his teeth tight over it. A vision of Alcatraz with the wind in tail and mane galloped back across his memory and staring bitterly down at the girl he reflected that it was she who had brought him face to face with the temptation of the outlaw horse.

Then he found that he was saying stupidly: "I'm sure sorry, Miss Jordan. But I guess being sorry don't help much."

"None at all. And—we won't talk any longer about it, if you please. The thing is done; another failure. Mr. Hervey will give you your pay. You can do the rest of your talking to him."

She lowered her head; she opened the book; she adjusted it carefully to the light streaming over her shoulder; she even summoned a faint smile of interest as though her thoughts were a thousand miles from this petty annoyance and back in the theme of the story. Perris, blind with rage, barely saw the details, barely heard the many-throated chuckle from the watchers across the patio. Never in his life had he so hungered to answer scorn with scorn but his hands were tied. Alcatraz he must have as truly as a starved man must have food; and to win Alcatraz he must live on the Jordan ranch. He could not speak, or even think, for that maddening laughter was growing behind him; then he saw the hand of Marianne, as she turned a page, tremble slightly. At that his voice came to him.

"Lady, I can't talk to Hervey."

She answered without looking up, and he hated her for it.

"Are you ashamed to face him?"

"I'm afraid to face him."

That, indeed, brought her head up and let him see all of her rage translated into cruel scorn.

"Really afraid? I don't suppose I should be surprised."

He accepted that badgering as martyrs accept the anguish of fire.

"I'm afraid that if I turn around and see him, Miss Jordan, I ain't going to stop at words."

The foreman acted before she could speak. The laughter across the patio had stopped at Perris' speech; plainly Hervey must not remain quiescent. He dropped his big hand on the shoulder of Perris.

"Look here, bucco," he growled, "You're tolerable much of a kid to use man-sized talk. Turn around."

He even drew Perris slightly towards him, but the latter persisted facing the girl even though his words were for the foreman. She was growing truly frightened.

"Tell Hervey to take his hand off me," said the horse-breaker. "He's old enough to know better!"

If his words needed amplification it could be found in the wolfish malevolence of his lean face or in the tremor which shook him; the thin space of a thought divided him from action. Marianne sprang from her chair. She knew enough of Hervey to understand that he could not swallow this insult in the presence of his cowpunchers. She knew also by the sudden compression of his lips and the white line about them that her foreman felt himself to be no match for this tigerish fighter. She thrust between them. Even in her excitement she noticed that Hervey's hand came readily from the shoulder of Perris. The older man stepped back with his hand on his gun, but in a burst of pitying comprehension she knew that it was the courage of hopelessness. She swung about on Perris, all her control gone, and the bitterness of a thousand aggravations and all her failures on the ranch poured out in words.

"I know your kind and despise it. You practice with your guns getting ready for your murders which you call fair fights. Fair fights! As well race a thoroughbred against a cowpony! You wrong a man and then bully him. That's Western fair play! But I swear to you, Mr. Perris, that if you so much as touch your weapon I'll have my men run you down and whip you out of the mountains!"

Her outbreak gave him, singularly, a more even poise. There was never a fighter who was not a nervous man; there was never a fighter who in a crisis was not suddenly calm.

"Lady," he answered, "you think you know the West, but you don't. If me and Hervey fell out there wouldn't be a man yonder across the patio that'd lift a hand till the fight was done. That ain't the Western way."

He had spoken much more than he was assured of. He had even sensed, behind him, the rising of the cowpunchers as the girl talked but at this appeal to their spirit of fair-play they settled down again.

He went on, speaking so that every man in the patio could hear: "If I won, they might tackle me one by one and we'd have it out till a better man beat me fair and square. But mobs don't jump one man, lady—not around these parts unless he's stole a hoss!"

"I don't ask no help," said Lew Hervey, but his voice was husky and uneven. "I'll stand my ground with any man, gun-fighter or not!"

"Please be quiet and let me handle this affair," said the girl. "As a matter of fact, it's ended. If you won't take the money from Mr. Hervey, I'll pay it to you myself. How much?"

"Nothing," said Red Perris.

"Are you going to give me an example of wounded virtue?" cried Marianne, white with contempt.

He was as pale as she, and taking off his hat he began to dent and re-dent its four sides. The girl, looking at that red shock of hair and the lowered eyes, guessed for the first time that he was suffering an agony of humiliation. Half of her anger instantly vanished and remembering her passion of the moment before, she began to wonder what she had said. In the meantime, shrugging his shoulders with a forced indifference, Hervey crossed the patio and she was aware that he was received in silence—no murmurs of congratulation for the manner in which he had borne himself during the interview.

"I got to ask you to gimme about two minutes of listening, Miss Jordan. Will you do it?"

"At least I won't stop you. Say what you please, Mr. Perris."

She wished heartily that she could have spoken with a little show of relenting but she had committed herself to coldness. In her soul of souls she wanted to bid him take a chair and tell her frankly all about it, assure him that after a moment of blind anger she had never doubted his straightforward desire to serve her. He began to speak.

"It's this way. I come out here to shoot a hoss, and I've worked tolerable hard to get in rifle range. I guess Hervey has been saying that I've got into shooting distance a dozen times but it ain't true. He happened to be sneaking about to-day, and he saw Alcatraz come close by me for the first time."

He paused. "I'll give you my word on that."

"You don't need to" said the girl, impetuously.

His eyes flashed up at her, at that, and he stood suddenly straight as though she had given him the right to stop cringing and talk like a man. What on earth, she wondered, could have forced the man to such humility? It made her shrink as one might on seeing an eagle cower before a wren. As for Perris, his resentment was in no wise abated by her friendliness. She had given him some moments of torture and the memory of that abasement would haunt him many a day. He mutely vowed that she should pay for it, and went on: "I sure wanted to sing when I caught Alcatraz in the sights. I pulled a bead on him just behind the shoulder but I could see the muscles along his shoulders working and it was a pretty sight, Miss Jordan."

She nodded, frowning in the intentness with which she followed him. She had thought of him as one with the careless, mischievous soul of a child but now, in quick, deep glances, she reached to profounder things.

"I held the bead," he kept repeating, his glance going blankly past her as he struggled to find words for the strange experience, "but then I saw his ribs going in and out. He was big where the cinches would run, you see, and I began to understand where he got that wind of his that never gives out. Besides, I somehow got to thinking about his heart under the ribs, lady, and I figured it kind of low to stop all the life in him with a bullet. So I swung my bead up along his neck—he's got a long neck and that means a long stride—till I came plump on his head, and just then he swung his head and gave me a look."

He breathed deeply, and then: "It was like jumping into cold water all of a sudden. I felt hollow inside. And then all at once I knew they'd never been a hoss like him in the mountains. I knew he was an outlaw. I knew he was plumb bad. But I knew he was a king, lady, and I couldn't no more shoot him that I could lie behind a bush and shoot a man." He was suddenly on fire.

"Looked to me like he was my hoss. Like he'd been planned for me. I wanted him terrible bad, the way you want things when you're a kid—the way you want Christmas the day before, when it don't seem like you could wait for tomorrow."

"But—he's a man-killer, Mr. Perris. I've seen it!"

His hand went out to her and she listened in utter amazement while he pleaded with all his heart in his voice.

"Lemme have a chance to make him my hoss, murders or not! Lemme stay here on the ranch and work, because they's no other good place for hunting him. I know you want them mares, but some day I'll get my rope on him and then I swear I'll break him or he'll break me. I'll break him, ride him to death, or he'll pitch me off and finish me liked he finished Cordova. But I know I can handle him. I sure feel it inside of me, lady! Pay? I don't want pay! I'll work for nothing. If I had a stake, I'd give it to you for a chance to keep on trying for him. I know I'm asking a pile. You want the mares and you can get them the minute Alcatraz is dropped with a bullet,—but I tell you straight, he's worth all of 'em—all six and more!"

A light came over his face. "Miss Jordan, lemme stay on and try my luck and if I get him and break him, I'll turn him over to you. And I tell you: he's the wind on four feet."

"You'll do all this and then give him to me when he's gentled and broken—if that can be done? Then why do you want him?"

"I want to show him that he's got a master. He's played with me and plumb fooled me all these weeks. I want to get on him and show him he's beat." His fierce joy in the thought was contagious. "I want to make him turn when I pull on the reins. I'll have him start when I want to start and stop when I want to stop. I'll make him glad when I talk soft to him and shake when I talk hard. He's made a fool of me; I'll make a fool and a show of him. Lady, will you say yes?"

He had swept her off her feet and with a mind full of a riot of imaginings—the frantic stallion, the clinging rider, the struggle for superiority—she breathed: "Yes, yes! A thousand times yes—and good luck, Mr. Perris."

He tossed his arms above his head and cried out joyously.

"Lady, it's more'n ten years of life to me!"

"But wait!" she said, suddenly aware of Hervey, lingering in the background. "I haven't the power to let you stay. It's Mr. Hervey who has authority while my father is away."

The lips of Red Jim twitched to a sneering malevolence mingled with gloom.

"It's up to him?" he echoed. "Then I might of spared myself all of this talk."

It would all be over in a moment. The foreman would utter the refusal. Red Perris would be in his saddle and bound towards the mountains. And that thought gave Marianne sudden insight into the fact that the Valley of the Eagles would be a drear, lonely place without Red Jim.

"You don't know Mr. Hervey," she broke in before the foreman could speak for himself. "He'll bear no malice to you. He's forgotten that squabble over—"

"Sure I have," said Lew Hervey. "I've forgotten ten all about it. But the way I figure, Miss Jordan, is that Perris is like a chunk of dynamite on the ranch. Any day one of the boys may run into him and there'll be a killing. They're red-hot against him. They might start for him in a gang one of these days, for all I know. For his own sake, Perris had better leave the Valley."

He had advanced his argument cunningly enough and by the way Marianne's eyes grew large and her color changed, he knew that he had made his point.

"Would they do that?" she gasped. "Have we such men?"

"I dunno," said Lew. "He sure rode 'em hard that morning."

"Then go," cried Marianne, turning eagerly to Red Jim. "For heaven's sake, go at once! Forget Alcatraz—forget the mares—but start at once, Mr. Perris!"

Even a blind man might have guessed many things from the tremor of her voice. Lew Hervey saw enough to make his eyes contract to the brightness of a ferret's as he glanced from the girl to handsome Jim Perris. But the red-headed adventurer was quite blind, quite deaf. No matter how the thing had been done, he knew that the girl and the foreman were now both combined to drive him from the ranch, from Alcatraz. For a moment of blind anger he wanted to crush, kill, destroy. Then he turned on his heel and strode towards the arch which led into the patio.

"Mind you!" called Lew Hervey in warning. "It's on your own head, Perris. If you don't leave, I'll throw you off!"

Red Jim flashed about under the shade of the arch.

"Come get me, and be damned," he said.

And then he was gone. The cowpunchers, furious at this open defiance of them all, boiled out into the patio, growling.

"You see?" said Hervey to the girl. "He won't be satisfied till there's a killing!"

"Keep them back!" she pleaded. "Don't let them go, Mr. Hervey. Don't let them follow him!"

One sharp, short order from Hervey stopped the foremost as they ran for the entrance. In fact, not one of them was peculiarly keen to follow such a trail as this in the darkness. Breathless silence fell over the patio, and then they heard the departing beat of the hoofs of Red's horse. And the shock of every footfall struck home in the heart of Marianne and filled her with a great loneliness and terror. And then the noise of the gallop died away in the far-off night.

CHAPTER XVII
INVISIBLE DANGER

ALCATRAZ, cresting the hill, warned the mares with a snort. One by one the bays brought up their beautiful heads to attention but the grey, as was her custom in moments of crisis or indecision, trotted forward to the side of the leader and glanced over the rolling lands below. Her decision was instant and decisive. She shook her head and turning to the side, she started down the left slope at a trot. Alcatraz called her back with another snort. He knew, as well as she did, the meaning of that faint odor on the east wind: it was man, unmistakably the great enemy; but during five days that scent had hung steadily here and yet, over all the miles which he could survey there was no sign of a man nor any places where man could be concealed. There was not a tree; there was not a fallen log; there was not a stump; there was not a rock of such respectable dimensions that even a rabbit would dare to seek shelter behind it. Still, mysteriously, the scent of man was there.

Alcatraz stamped with impatience and when the grey whinnied he merely shook his head angrily in answer. It irritated him to have her always right, always cautious, and besides he felt somewhat shamed by the necessity of using her as a court of last appeal. To be sure, he was a keener judge of the sights and scents of the mountain desert than any of the half-bred mares but though he lived to fifty years he would never approach the stored wisdom, the uncanny acuteness of eye, ear, and nostril of the wild grey. Her view-point seemed, at times, that of the high-sailing buzzards, for she guessed, miles and miles away, what water-holes were dry and what "tanks" brimmed with water; what trails were broken by landslides since they had last been travelled and where new trails might be found or made; when it was wise to seek shelter because a sand-storm was brewing; where the grass grew thickest and most succulent on far-off hillsides; and so on and on the treasury of her knowledge could be delved in inexhaustibly.

On only one point did he feel that his cleverness might rival hers and that point was the most important of all—man the Great Destroyer. She knew him only from a distance whereas had not Alcatraz breathed that dreaded scent close at hand? Had he not on one unforgetable occasion felt the soft flesh turn to pulp beneath his stamping feet, and heard the breaking of bones? His nostrils distended at the memory and again he searched the lowlands.

No, there was not a shadow of a place where man might be concealed and that scent could be nothing but a snare and an illusion. To be sure there were other ways hardly less convenient to the waterhole, but why should he be turned from the easiest way day after day because of this unbodied warning? He started down the slope.

It brought the grey after him, neighing wildly, but though she circled around him at full speed time after time, he would not pause, and when she attempted to block him he raised his head and pushed her away with the resistless urge of breast and shoulders. At that she attempted no more forceful persuasion but fell in behind him, still pausing from time to time to send her mournfully persuasive whinny after the obdurate leader until even the bays, usually so blindly docile, grew alarmed and fell back to a huddled grouping half way between Alcatraz and the trailing grey. It touched his pride sharply, this division of their trust. Twice he slackened his lope and called to them to hasten and when they responded with only a faint-hearted trot he was forced to mask his impatience. Coming to a walk he cropped imaginary grasses from time to time and so induced the others to draw nearer.

It was slow work going down the hollow in this way, and hot work, too, but though he often glanced up yearningly towards the wooded hills beyond, he kept to his pretense of carelessness and so managed to hold the mares in a close-bunched group behind him. In the meantime the scent grew stronger, closer to the ground on that east wind. Time and again he raised his head and stared earnestly, but it was impossible for any living creature to stalk within hundreds of yards of him without being seen—whereas that scent spoke of one almost within leaping distance. Once it seemed to his excited imagination—as he lowered his head to sniff at a tuft of dead grasses—that he heard the sound of human breathing.

He snorted the foolish thought into nothingness and after a glance back to make sure that his companions followed, he resolutely stepped out into the very heart of the man-scent. So closely was that phantom located by the sense of smell that it seemed to Alcatraz he could see the exact spot on the hillside behind a small rock where the ghost must lie. Yet he disdained to flee from empty air and for all his beating heart he raised his head and walked sedately on. The danger spot was drifting past on his left when a squeal of fear from the wild grey far in the rear made Alcatraz leap sidewise with catlike suddenness.

Growing by magic from the sand behind the little rock the head and shoulders of a man appeared, his shadow pouring down the sun-whitened slope. In his hand he swung a rapidly lengthening loop of rope and as his arm went back it knocked off the fellow's hat and exposed a shock of red hair. So much Alcatraz saw while the paralysis of fear locked every joint for the tenth part of a second, and deeply as he dreaded the apparition itself he dreaded more the whipping circle of rope. For had he not seen the dead thing become alive and snakelike in the skilled hand of Manuel Cordova? The freezing terror relaxed; the sand crunched away under the drive of his rear hoofs as he flung himself forward—with firm footing to aid he would have slid from beneath the flying danger, but as it was he heard the live rope whisper in the air above his head.

He landed on stiff legs, checked his forward impetus and flung sidewise. On solid footing he would have dodged successfully; as it was the noose barely clipped past his ear.

As the rope touched his neck, it seemed to Alcatraz that every wound dealt him by the hand of man was suddenly aching and bleeding again, the skin along his flanks quivered where the spurs of Cordova had driven home time and again, and on shoulders and belly and hips there were burning stripes where the quirt had raised its wale. Most horrible of all, in his mouth came the taste of iron and his own blood where the Spanish bit had wrenched his jaws apart. Out of the old days he might have remembered the first and bitterest lesson—that it is folly to pull against a rope—but now he saw nothing save the fleeing forms of the seven mares and his own freedom vanishing with them. In his mid-leap the lariat hummed taut, sank in a burning circle into the flesh at the base of his neck, and he was flung to the ground. No man's power could have stopped him so short; the cunning enemy had turned a half-hitch around the top of that deep-rooted rock.

He landed, not inert, but shocked out of hysteria into all his old cunning—that wily savagery which had kept Cordova in fear, ten-fold more terrible since the free life had clothed him with his full strength. The very impetus of his fall he used to help him whirl to his feet, and as he rose he knew what he must do. To struggle against the tools of man was always madness and brought only pain as a result; like a good general he determined to end the battle by getting at the root of the enemy's fire, and wheeling on his hind legs he charged Red Perris.

The first leap revealed the mystery of the man's appearance. Behind this rock, which was barely sufficient shelter for his head, he had excavated a pit sufficient to shelter his crouching body and the sand which he removed for this purpose had been spread evenly over the slope so that no suspicion might be created in the most watchful eye. He had sprung from his concealment and was now working to loosen the half-hitch from the rock. As the knot came free Alcatraz was turning and now Perris faced the charge with the rope caught in his hand. What could he do? There was only one thing, and the stallion saw the heavy revolver bared and levelled at him, a flickering bit of metal. He knew well what it meant but there was no hope save to rush on; another stride and he would be on that frail creature, tearing with his teeth and crushing with his hoofs. And then a miracle happened. The revolver was flung aside, a gleaming arc and a splash of sand where it struck; Red Perris preferred to risk his life rather than end the battle before it was well begun with a bullet. He crouched over the rope as though he had braced himself to meet the shock of the charging stallion. But that was not his purpose. As the stallion rushed on him he darted to one side and the fore hoof with which Alcatraz struck merely slashed his shirt down the back.

A feint had saved him, but Alcatraz was no bull to charge blindly twice. He checked himself so abruptly that he knocked up a shower of sand, and he turned savagely out of that dust-cloud to end the struggle. Yet this small, mad creature stood his ground, showed no inclination to flee. With the rope he was doing strange things, making it spin in swift spirals, close to the ground. Let him do what he would, his days were ended. Alcatraz bared his teeth, laid back his ears, and lunged again. Another miracle! As his forefeet struck the ground in the midst of one of those wide circles of rope, the red-headed man lunged back, the circle jumped like a living thing and coiled itself around both forefeet, between fetlock and hoof. When he attempted the next leap his front legs crumbled beneath him. At the very feet of Red Perris he plunged into the sand.

Once more he whirled to regain his lost footing, but as he turned on his back the rope twisted and whispered above him; the off hind leg was noosed, and then the near one—Alcatraz lay on his side straining and snorting but utterly helpless.

Of a sudden he ceased all struggle. About neck and all four hoofs was the burning grip of the rope, so bitterly familiar, and man had once again enslaved him. Alcatraz relaxed. Presently there would come a swift volley of curses, then the whir and cut of the whip—no, for a great occasion such as this the man would choose a large and durable club and beat him across the ribs. Why not? Even as he had served Cordova this man of the flaming hair would now serve him. He was very like Cordova in one thing. He did not hurry, but first picked up his revolver and replaced it in its holster, having blown the sand from the mechanism as well as he could. Then he put on his fallen hat and stood back with his hands dropped on his hips and eyed the captive. For the first time he spoke, and Alcatraz shuddered at the sound of a voice well-nigh as smooth as that of Cordova, with the same well-known ring of fierce exultation.

"God A'mighty, God A'mighty! They can't be no hoss like this! Jim, you're dreaming. Rub your fool eyes and wake up!"

He began to walk in a circle about his victim, and Alcatraz shuddered when the conqueror came behind him. That had been Cordova's way—to come to a place where he could not be seen and then strike cruelly and by surprise. To his unspeakable astonishment, Perris presently leaned over him—and then deliberately sat down on the shoulder of the chestnut. Two thoughts flashed through the mind of the stallion; he might heave himself over by a convulsive effort and attempt to crush this insolent devil; or he might jerk his head around and catch Perris with his teeth. A third and better thought, however, immediately followed—that bound as he was he would have little chance to reach this elusive will-o'-the-wisp. He could not repress a quiver of horror and anger, but beyond that he did not stir.

Other liberties were being taken; Cordova in his maddest moments would not have dared so much. Down the long muscles of his shoulder and upper foreleg went curious and gently prying finger-tips, and where they passed a tingling sensation followed, not altogether unpleasant. Again beginning on his neck the hand trailed down beneath his mane and at the same time the voice was murmuring: "Oh beauty! Oh beauty!"

The heart of Alcatraz swelled. He had felt his first caress.

CHAPTER XVIII
VICTORY

NOT that he recognized it as such but the touch was a pleasure and the quiet voice passed into his mind with a mild and soothing influence that made the wide freedom of the mountain-desert seem a worthless thing. The companionship of the mares was a bodiless nothing compared with the hope of feeling that hand again, hearing that voice, and knowing that all troubles, all worries were ended for ever. Like the stout Odysseus of many devices Alcatraz scorned the ways of the lotus eaters; for well he knew how Cordova had often lured him to perfect trust with the magic of man's voice, only to waken him from the dream of peace with the sting of a blacksnake. This red-headed man, so soft of hand, so pleasant of voice, was for those very reasons the more to be suspected. The chestnut bided his time; presently the torment would begin.

The calm voice was proceeding: "Old sport, you and me are going to stage a sure enough scrap right here and now. Speaking personal, I'd like to take off the rope and go at you man to man with no saddle to help me out. But if I did that I wouldn't have a ghost of a show. I'll saddle you, right enough, but I'll ride you without spurs, and I'll put a straight bit in your mouth—damn the Mexican soul of Cordova, I see where he's sawed your mouth pretty near in two with his Spanish contraptions! Without a quirt or spurs or a curb to choke you down, you and me'll put on a square fight, so help me God! Because I think I can beat you, old hoss. Here goes!"

The stallion listened to the soothing murmur, listened and waited, and sure enough he had not long to stay in expectation. For Perris went to the hole behind the rock and presently returned carrying that flapping, creaking instrument of torture—a saddle.

To all that followed—the blind-folding, the bridling, the jerk which urged him to his feet, the saddling,—Alcatraz submitted with the most perfect docility. He understood now that he was to have a chance to fight for his liberty on terms of equality and his confidence grew. In the old days that consummate horseman, Manuel Cordova, had only been able to keep his seat by underfeeding Alcatraz to the point of exhaustion but now, from withers to fetlock joint, the chestnut was conscious of a mighty harmony of muscles and reserves of energy. The wiles which he had learned in many a struggle with the Mexican were not forgotten and the tricks which had so often nearly unseated the old master could now be executed with threefold energy. In the meantime he waited quietly, assuming an air of the most perfect meekness, with the toe of one hind foot pointed so that he sagged wearily on that side, and with his head lowered in all the appearance of mild subjection.

The cinches bit deep into his flesh. He tasted that horror of iron in his mouth, with this great distinction: that whereas the bits of Manuel Cordova had been heavy instruments of torture this was a light thing, smooth and straight and without the wheel of spikes. The crisis was coming. He felt the weight of the rider fall on the left stirrup, the reins were gathered, then Perris swung lightly into the saddle and leaning, snatched the blindfold from the eyes of the stallion.

One instant Alcatraz waited for the sting of the spurs, the resounding crack of the heavy quirt, the voice of the rider raised in curses; but all was silence. The very feel of the man in the saddle was different, not so much in poundage as in a certain exquisite balance which he maintained but the pause lasted no longer than a second after the welcome daylight flashed on the eyes of Alcatraz. Fear was a spur to him, fear of the unknown. He would have veritably welcomed the brutalities of Cordova simply because they were familiar—but this silent and clinging burden? He flung himself high in the air, snapped up his back, shook himself in mid-leap, and landed with every leg stiff. But a violence which would have hurled another man to the ground left Perris laughing. And were beasts understood, that laughter was a shameful mockery!

Alcatraz thrust out his head. In vain Perris tugged at the reins. The lack of curb gave him no pry on the jaw of the chestnut and sheer strength against strength he was a child on a giant. The strips of leather burned through his fingers and the first great point of the battle was decided in favor of the horse: he had the bit in his teeth. It was a vital advantage for, as every one knows who has struggled with a pitching horse, it cannot buck with abandon while its chin is tucked back against its breast; only when the head is stretched out and the nose close to the ground can a bucking horse double back and forth to the full of his agility, twisting and turning and snapping as an "educated" bucker knows how.

And Alcatraz knew, none so well! The deep exclamation of dismay from the rider was sweetest music to his malicious ears, and, in sheer joy of action, he rushed down the hollow at full speed, bucking "straight" and with never a trick attempted, but when the first ecstasy cleared from his brain he found that Perris was still with him, riding light as a creature of mist rather than a solid mass of bone and muscle—in place of jerking and straining and wrenching, in place of plying the quirt or clinging with the tearing spurs, he was riding "straight up" and obeying every rule of that unwritten code which prescribes the manner in which a gentleman cowpuncher shall combat with his horse for superiority. Again that thrill of terror of the unknown passed through the stallion; could this apparently weaponless enemy cling to him in spite of his best efforts? He would see, and that very shortly. Without going through the intermediate stages by which the usual educated bronco rises to a climax of his efforts, Alcatraz began at once that most dreaded of all forms of bucking—sun-fishing. The wooded hills were close now and the ground beneath him was firm underfoot assuring him full use of all his agility and strength. His motion was like that of a breaking comber. First he hurled himself into the air, then pitched sharply down and landed on one stiffened foreleg—the jar being followed by the deadly whiplash snap to the side as he slumped over. Then again driven into the air by the impulse of those powerful hind legs, he landed on the alternate foreleg and snapped his rider in the opposite direction—a blow on the base of the brain and another immediately following on the side.

Underfed mustangs have killed men by this maneuver, repeated without end.

Alcatraz was no starveling mongrel, but to the fierceness of a wild horse and the tireless durability of a mustang he united the subtlety which he had gained in his long battle with the Mexican and above all this, his was the pride of one who had already conquered man. His fierce assault began to produce results.

He saw Red Perris sway drunkenly at every shock; his head seemed to swing on a pivot from side to side under that fearful jolting—his mouth was ajar, his eyes staring, a fearful mask of a face; yet he clung in place. When he was stunned, instinct still kept his feet in the stirrups and taught him to give lightly to every jar. He fought hard but in time even Red Perris must collapse.

But could the attack be sustained indefinitely? Grim as were results of sun-fishing on the rider, they were hardly less vitiating for the horse. The forelegs of Alcatraz began to grow numb below the shoulder; his knees bowed and refused to give the shock its primal snap; to the very withers he was an increasing ache. He must vary the attack. As soon as that idea came, he reared and flung himself back to the earth.

He heard a sharp exclamation from the rider—he felt the tug as the right foot of Perris hung in the stirrup, then the stunning impact on the ground. To make sure of his prey he whirled himself to the left, but even so his striking feet did not reach the Great Enemy. Perris had freed himself in the last fraction of a second and pitching headlong from the saddle he rolled over and over in the dirt, safe. That fall opened a new hope to Alcatraz. Had he possessed his full measure of agility he would have gained his feet and rushed the man, but the long struggle had taken the edge from his activity and as he lunged up he saw Perris, springing almost on all-fours, animal-like, leap through the air and his weight struck home in the saddle.

Quick, now, before the Enemy gained a secure hold, before that reaching foot attained the other stirrup, before the proper balance was struck! Up in the air went the chestnut—down on one stiff foreleg and with a great swelling of the heart he felt the rider slump far to one side, clinging with one leg from the saddle, one hand wrapped in the flying mane. Now victory with a last effort! Again he leaped high and again struck stiffly on the opposite foreleg; but alas! that very upward bound swung Perris to the erect, and with incredible and catlike speed he slipped into the saddle. He received the shock with both feet lodged again in the supporting stirrups.

The frenzy of disappointment gave Alcatraz renewed energy. It was not sun-fishing now, but fence-rowing, cross-bucking, flinging himself to the earth again and again, racing a little distance and stopping on braced legs, sun-fishing to end the programme. As he fought he watched results. It was as though invisible fists were crashing against the head and body of the unfortunate rider. From nose and ears and gaping mouth the blood trickled; his eyes were blurs of red; his head rolled hideously on his shoulders. Ten times he was saved by a hair's-breadth from a fall; ten times he righted himself again and a strange and bubbling voice jerked out defiance to the horse.

"Buck—damn you!—go it, you devil—I'll—beat—you still! I'll break you—I'll—make you come—when I whistle—I'll make you—a—lady's hoss!"'

Consuming terror was in the stallion and the fear that, incredible as it seemed, he was being beaten by a man who did not use man's favorite weapon—pain. No, not once had the cruel spurs clung in his flanks, or the quirt whirred and fallen; not once, above all, had his mouth been torn and his jaw nearly broken by the wrenching of a curb. It came vaguely into the brutes' mind that there was something to be more dreaded than either bit, spur, or whip, and that was the controlling mind which spoke behind the voice of Perris, which was telegraphed again and again down the taut reins. That fear as much as the labor drained his vigor.

His knees buckled now. He could no longer sunfish. He could not even buck straight with the bone-breaking energy. He was nearly done, with a tell-tale wheeze in his lungs, with blood pressure making his eyes start well-nigh from his head, and a bloody froth choking him. Red Perris also was in the last stage of exhaustion—one true pitch would have hurled him limp from his seat—yet, with his body numb from head to toe, he managed to keep his place by using that last and greatest strength of feeble man—power of will. Alcatraz, coming at last to a beaten stop, looked about him for help.

There was nothing to aid, nothing save the murmur of the wind in the trees just before him. Suddenly his ears pricked with new hope and he shut out the weak voice which murmured huskily: "I've got you now. I've got you, Alcatraz. I've all by myself—no whip,—no spur—no leather pulling—I've rode straight up and——"

Alcatraz lunged out into a rickety gallop. Only new hope sustained him as he headed straight for the trees.

Even the dazed brain of Perris understood. With all his force he wrenched at the bit—it was hopelessly lodged in the teeth of the stallion—and then he groaned in despair and a moment later swayed forward to avoid a bough brushing close overhead.

There were other branches ahead. On galloped Alcatraz, heading cunningly beneath the boughs until he was stopped by a shock that dropped him staggering to his knees. The pommel had struck a branch—and Red Perris was still in place.

Once more the chestnut started, reeling heavily in his lope. This time, to avoid the coming peril, the rider slipped far to one side and Alcatraz veered swiftly towards a neighboring tree trunk. Too late Red Perris saw the danger and strove to drag himself back into the saddle, but his numbed muscles refused to act and Alcatraz felt the burden torn from his back, felt a dangling foot tug at the left stirrup—then he was free.

So utter was his exhaustion that in checking himself he nearly fell, but he turned to look at the mischief he had worked.

The man lay on his back with his arms flung out cross-wise. From a gash in his forehead the blood streamed across his face. His legs were twisted oddly together. His eyes were closed. From head to foot the stallion sniffed that limp body, then raised a forehoof to strike; with one blow he could smash the face to a smear of red as he had smashed Manuel Cordova the great day long before.

The hoof fell, was checked, and wondering at himself Alcatraz found that his blow had not struck home. What was it that restrained him? It seemed to the conqueror that he felt again the gentle finger-tips which had worked down the muscles of his shoulder and trailed down his neck. More than that, he heard the smooth murmur of the man's voice like a kindly ghost beside him. He dreaded Red Perris still, but hate the fallen rider he could not. Presently a loud rushing of the wind among the branches above made him turn and in a panic he left the forest at a shambling trot.

CHAPTER XIX
HERVEY TAKES A TRICK

THE night before, when Perris rode off from the ranchhouse after defying Hervey and his men, his hoofbeats had no sooner faded to nothing than the cowpunchers swarmed out from the patio and into the open; as though they wished to put their heads together and plan the battle which the command of Hervey, to-night, had postponed. All of that was perfectly clear to Marianne. Her call brought Hervey back to her and she led him at once off the veranda and to the living room where she could talk secure of interruption or of being overheard. There he slumped uninvited into the first easy chair and sat twirling his sombrero on his finger-tips, obviously well satisfied with himself and the events of the evening. She herself remained standing, carefully turning her back to the light so that her face might, as much as possible, be in shadow. For she knew it was pale and the eyes unnaturally large.

Hervey must not see. He must not guess at the torment in her mind and all the self-revelations which had been pouring into her consciousness during the past few moments. Greatest of all was one overshadowing fact: she loved Red Jim Perris! What did it matter that she had seen him so few times, and spoke to him so few words? A word might be a thunderclap; a glance might carry into the very soul of a man. And indeed she felt that she had seen that proud, gay, impatient soul in Jim. What he thought of her was another matter. That he found a bar between them was plain. But on the night of his first arrival at the ranch, when she sang to him, had she not felt him, once, twice and again, leaning towards her, into her life. And if they met once more, might he not come all the way? But no matter. The thing now was to use all her cunning of mind, all her strength of body, to save him from imminent danger; and the satisfied glint of Hervey's eye convinced her that the danger was imminent indeed. Why he should hate Jim so bitterly was not clear; that he did so hate the stranger was self-evident. The more she studied her foreman the more her terror grew, the more her lonely sense of weakness increased.

"Mr. Hervey," she said suddenly. "What's to be done?"

Her heart fell. He had avoided her eyes.

"I dunno," said Hervey. "You seen to-night that I treated him plumb white. I put my cards on the table. I warned him fair and square. And that after I'd given him a week's grace. A gent couldn't do any more than that, I guess!"

He was right, in a way. At least, the whole populace of the mountains would agree that he had given Red Jim every chance to leave the ranch peaceably. And if he would not go peaceably, who could raise a finger against Hervey for throwing the man off by force?

"But something more *has* to be done," she said eagerly. "It *has* to be done!"

Hervey frowned at her.

"Look here," he said, in a more dictatorial manner than he had ever used before. "Why you so interested in this Perris?"

She hesitated, but only for an instant. What did such a thing as shame matter when the life of Perris might be saved by a confession? And certainly Hervey would not dare to proceed against Perris if she made such a confession.

"I'm interested," she said steadily, "because he—he means more to me than any other man in the world."

She saw the head of the foreman jerk back as though he had received a blow in the face.

"More'n your father?"

"In a different way—yes, more than Dad!"

Hervey rose and stretched an accusing arm towards her.

"You're in love with Red Perris!"

And she answered him fiercely: "Yes, yes, yes! In love with Red Perris! Go tell every one of your men. Shame me as far as you wish! But—Mr. Hervey, you won't dare lead a gang against him now!"

He drew back from her, thrust away by her half-hysteria of emotion.

"Won't I?" growled Hervey, regarding her from beneath sternly gathered brows. "I seen something of this to-night. I guessed it all. Won't I lay a hand on a sneaking hound that comes grinning and talking soft and saying things he don't half mean? Why, it's a better reason for throwing him off the ranch than I ever had before, seems to me!"

"You don't mean that!" she breathed. "Say you don't mean that!"

"Your Dad ain't here. If he was, he'd say the same as me. I got to act in his place. You think you like Perris. Why, you'd be throwing yourself away. You'd break Oliver Jordan's heart. That's what you'd do!"

Her brain was whirling. She grasped at the first thought that came to her.

"Then wait till he comes back before you touch Jim Perris."

"And let Perris raise the devil in the meantime?"

He laughed in her face.

"At least," she cried, her voice shrill with anger and fear, "let me know where he is. Let me send for him myself."

"Dunno that I'm exactly sure about where he is myself," fenced Lew Hervey.

"Ah," moaned the girl, half-breaking down under the strain. "Why do you hate me so? What have I done to you?"

"Nothing," said Hervey grimly. "Made me the laughing stock of the mountains—that's all. Made me a joke—that's all you've done to me. 'Lew Hervey and his boss—the girl.' That's what they been saying about me. But I ain't been taking that to heart. What I'm doing now is for your own good, only you don't know it! You'll see it later on."

"Mr. Hervey," she pleaded, "if it will change you, I'll give you my oath to stop bothering with the management of the ranch. You can run it your own way. I'll leave if you say the word, but——"

"I know," said Hervey. "I know what you'd say. But Lord above, Miss Jordan, I ain't doing this for my own sake. I'm doing it for yours and your father's. He'll thank me if you don't! Far as Perris goes, I'd——"

He halted. She had sunk into a chair—collapsed into it, rather, and lay there half fainting with one arm thrown across her face. Hervey glowered down on her a moment and then turned on his heel and left the house.

He went straight to the bunkhouse, gathered the men about him, and told them the news.

"Boys," he said, "the cat's out of the bag. I've found out everything, and it's what I been fearing. She started begging me to keep off Red Jim's trail. Wouldn't hear no reason. I told her there wasn't nothing for me to gain by throwing him off the ranch. Except that he'd been ordered off and he had to go. It'd make a joke of me and all of you boys if the word got around that one gent had laughed at us and stayed right in the Valley when we told him to get out."

A fierce volley of curses bore him out.

"Well," said Hervey, "then she come right out and told me the truth: she's in love with Perris. She told me so herself!"

They gaped at him. They were young enough, most of them, and lonely and romantic enough, to have looked on Marianne with a sort of sad longing which their sense of humor kept from being anything more aspiring. But to think that she had given her heart so suddenly and so freely to this stranger was a shock. Hervey reaped the harvest of their alarmed glances with a vast inward content. Every look he met was an incipient gun levelled at the head of Red Jim.

"Didn't make no bones about it," he said, "she plumb begged for him. Well, boys, she ain't going to get him. I think too much of old man Jordan to let his girl run off with a man-killing vagabond like this Perris. He's good looking and he talks dead easy. That's what's turned the trick. I guess the rest of you would back me up?"

The answer was a growl.

"I'll go bust his neck," said Little Joe furiously. "One of them heart-breakers, I figure."

"First thing," said the foreman, "is to see that she don't get to him. If she does, she'll sure run off with him. But she's easy kept from that. Joe, you and Shorty watch the hoss corrals to-night, will you? And don't let her get through to a hoss by talking soft to you."

They vowed that they would be adamant. They vowed it with many oaths. In fact, the rage of the cowpunchers was steadily growing. Red Perris was more than a mere insolent interloper who had dared to scoff at the banded powers of the Valley of the Eagles. He was far worse. He was the most despicable sort of sneak and thief for he was trying to steal the heart and ruin the life of a girl. They had looked upon the approaching conflict with Perris as a bitter pill that must be swallowed for the sake of the Valley of the Eagles outfit. They looked upon it, from this moment, as a religious duty from which no one with the name of a man dared to shrink. Little Joe and Shorty at once started for the corral. The others gathered around the foreman for further details, but he waved them away and retired to his own bunk. For he never used the little room at the end of the building which was set aside for the foreman. He lived and slept and ate among his cowpunchers and that was one reason for his hold over them.

At his bunk, he produced writing materials scribbled hastily.

"Dear Jordan,

"Hell has busted loose.

"I played Perris with a long rope. I gave him a week because Miss Jordan asked me to. But at the end of the week he still wasn't ready to go. Seems that he's crazy to get Alcatraz. Talks about the horse like a drunk talking about booze. Plumb disgusting. But when I told him to go to-night, he up and said they wasn't enough men in the Valley to throw him off the ranch. I would of taken a fall out of him for that, but Miss Jordan stepped in and kept me away from him.

"Afterwards I had a talk with her. She begged me not to go after Perris because he would fight and that meant a killing. I told her I had to do what I'd said I'd do. Then she busted out and told me that she loved Perris. Seemed to think that would keep me from going after Perris. She might of knowed that it was the very thing that would make me hit the trail. I'm not going to stand by and see a skunk like Perris run away with your girl while you ain't on the ranch.

"I've just given orders to a couple of the boys to see that she don't get a horse to go out to Perris. Tomorrow or the next day I'll settle his hash.

"This letter may make you think that you'd better come back to the ranch. But take my advice and stay off. I can handle this thing better while you're away. If you're here you'll have to listen to a lot of begging and crying. Come back in a week and everything will be cleared up.

"Take it easy and don't worry none. I'm doing my best for you and your daughter, even if she don't know it.

"Sincerely,

"LEW HERVEY."

This letter, when completed, he surveyed with considerable complacence. If ever a man were being bound to another by chains of inseparable gratitude, Oliver Jordan was he! Indeed, the whole affair was working out so smoothly, so perfectly, that Hervey felt the thrill of an artist sketching a large and harmonious composition. In the first place, Red Jim Perris, whom he hated with unutterable fervor because the younger man filled him with dread, would be turned, as Hervey expressed it, "into buzzard food." And Hervey would be praised for the act! Oliver Jordan, owing the preservation of his daughter from a luckless marriage to the vigilance of his foreman, could never regret the life-contract which he had drawn up. No doubt that contract, as it stood, could never hold water in the law. But Jordan's gratitude would make it proof. Last of all, and best of all, when Perris was disposed of, Marianne would never be able to remain on the ranch. She would go to forget her sorrow among her school friends in the East. And Hervey, undisputed lord and master of the ranch, could bleed it white in half a dozen years and leave it a mere husk, overladen with mortgages.

No wonder a song was in the heart of the foreman as he sealed the letter. He gave the message to Slim, and added directions.

"You'll be missing from the party," he said, as he handed over the letter, "but the party we have with Perris is apt to be pretty much like a party with a wild-cat. You can thank your stars you'll be on the road when it comes off!"

And Slim had sense enough to nod in agreement.

CHAPTER XX
THE TRAP SHUTS

IN one matter Lew Hervey had acted none too quickly. Shorty and Little Joe arrived at the corral in time to find Marianne in the very act of leading out her pony. They told her firmly and gently that the horse must go back, and when she defied them, they astonished her by simply removing her hand from the lead-rope and taking the horse away. In vain she stormed and threatened. In vain, at length, she broke into tears. Either of them would have given an arm to serve her. But in fact they considered they were at that moment rendering the greatest service possible. They were saving her from herself.

She fled back to the house again, finally, and threw herself face down on her bed in an agony of dread, and helplessness, and shame. Shame because from Little Joe's brief remarks, she gathered that Hervey had already spread the news of her confession. But shame and fear were suddenly forgotten. She found herself sitting wide-eyed on the edge of the bed repeating over and over in a shaking voice "I have to get there! I have to get there!"

But how utterly Hervey had tied her hands! She could not budge to warn Perris or to join him!

The long night wore away with Marianne crouched at the window straining her eyes towards the corrals. Night was the proper time for such a thing as the murder of Red Perris. They would not dare, she felt, for all their numbers, to face him in the honest sunshine. So she peered eagerly towards the shadowy outlines of the barns and sheds until at length a wan moon rose and gave her blessed light.

But no one approached the corrals from the bunkhouse, and at length, when the dawn began to grow, she fell asleep. It was a sleep filled with nightmares and before the sun was well up she was awake again, and at watch.

Mid-morning came, yet still none of the men rode out to their ordinary work. There could be only one meaning. They were held back to join the expedition. They were at this very moment, perhaps, cleaning their guns in the bunkhouse. Noon brought no action. They trooped cheerfully towards the house in answer to the noon-gong. She heard them laughing and jesting. What cold-blooded fiends they were to be able to conduct themselves in this manner when they intended to do a murder before the day had ended! And indeed, it was only for this meal they seemed to have planned to wait.

Before the afternoon was well begun, there was saddling and mounting and then Hervey, Little Joe, Shorty, Macintosh, and Scotty climbed onto their mounts and jogged out towards the east. Her heart leaped with only a momentary hope when she saw the direction, but instantly she undeceived herself. They would, of course, swing north as soon as they were well out of sight from the house, and then they would head for the shack on the mountainside, aiming to reach it at about the fall of twilight. And what could she do to stop them?

She ran out through the patio and to the front of the house. The dust-cloud already had swallowed the individual forms of the riders. And turning to the left, she saw McGuire and Hastings lolling in full view near the corrals. With consummate tact, Hervey had chosen those of his men who were the oldest, the hardest, the least liable to be melted by her persuasions.

Moaning, she turned back and looked east. The dust-cloud was dwindling every minute. And without hope, she cast another glance towards the corrals. Evidently, the men agreed that it was unnecessary for two of them to stay in the heat of the sun to prevent her from getting at a horse. Hastings had turned his back and was strolling towards the bunkhouse. McGuire was perched on a stump rolling a cigarette and grinning broadly towards her.

He would be a hard man to handle. But at least there was more hope than before. One man was not so hard to manage as two, each shaming the other into indifference. She went slowly towards McGuire, turning again to see the dust-cloud roll out of view over a distant hill.

In that cloud of dust, Hervey kept the pace down to an easy dog-trot. From mid-afternoon until evening—for he did not intend to expose himself primarily and his men in the second place, to the accurate gun of Red Jim in broad daylight—was a comfortable stretch in which to make the journey to the shack on the mountain-side. Like a good general, he kept the minds of his followers from growing tense by deftly turning the talk, on the way, to other topics, as they swung off the east trail towards Glosterville and journeyed due north over the rolling foothills. There was only one chance in three that he could have deceived the girl by his first direction, but that chance was worth taking. He had a wholesome respect for the mental powers of Oliver Jordan's daughter and he by no means wished to drive her frantic in the effort to get to Perris with her warning. Of course it would be impossible for her to wheedle McGuire and Hastings into letting her have a horse, but if she should——

Here Hervey abruptly turned his thoughts in a new direction. The old one led to results too unpleasant.

In the meantime, as they wore out the miles and the day turned towards sunset time, the cheery conversation which Little Joe had led among the riders fell away. They were coming too close to the time and place of action. What that action must be was only too easy to guess. It was simply impossible to imagine Red Perris submitting to an order to leave. He had already defied their assembled forces once. He would certainly make the attempt again. Of course odds of five to one were too great for even the most courageous and skilful fighter to face. But he might do terrible damage before the end.

And it was a solemn procession which wound up the hillside through the darkening trees. Until at length, at a word from Hervey, they dismounted, tethered their horses here and there where there was sufficient grass to occupy them and keep them from growing nervous and neighing, and then started on again on foot.

At this point Hervey took the lead. For that matter, he had never been lacking in sheer animal courage, and now he wound up the path with his long colt in his hand, ready to shoot, and shoot to kill. Once or twice small sounds made him pause, uneasy. But his progress was fairly steady until he came to the edge of the little clearing where the shack stood.

There was no sign of life about it. The shack seemed deserted. Thick darkness filled its doorway and the window, though the rest of the clearing was still permeated with a faint afterglow of the sunset.

"He ain't here," said Little Joe softly, as he came to the side of the watchful foreman.

"Don't be too sure," said the other. "I'd trust this Perris and take about as many chances with him as I would with a rattler in a six-by-six room. Maybe he's in there playing possum. Waiting for us to make a break across the clearing. That'd be fine for Red Jim, damn his heart!"

Little Joe peered back at the anxious faces of the others, as they came up the path one by one. He did not like to be one of so large a party held up by a single man. In fact, Joe was a good deal of a warrior himself. He was new to the Valley of the Eagles, but there were other parts of the mountain-desert where his fame was spread broadcast. There were even places where sundry officers of the law would have been glad to lay hands upon him.

"Well," quoth Joe, "we'll give him a chance. If he ain't a fighting man, but just a plain murderer, we'll let him show it," and so saying, he stepped boldly out from the sheltering darkness of the trees and strode towards the hut, an immense and awesome figure in the twilight.

Lew Hervey followed at once. It would not do to be out-dared by one of his crew in a crisis as important as this. But for all his haste the long strides of Joe had brought him to the door of the hut many yards in the lead, and he disappeared inside. Presently his big voice boomed: "He ain't here. Plumb vanished."

They gathered in the hut at once.

"Where's he gone?" asked the foreman, scratching his head.

"Maybe he ain't acting as big as he talked," said Shorty. "Maybe he's slid over the mountains."

"Strike a light, somebody," commanded the foreman.

Three or four sulphur matches were scratched at the same moment on trousers made tight by cocking the knee up. Each match glimmered through sheltering fingers with dull blue light, for a moment, and then as the sulphur was exhausted and the flame caught the wood, the hands opened and directed shafts of light here and there. The whole cabin was dimly illumined for a moment while man after man thrust his burning match towards something he had discovered.

"Here's his blankets. All mussed up."

"Here's a pair of boots."

"Here's the frying pan right on the stove."

They wandered here and there, lighting new matches until Little Joe spoke.

"No use, boys," he declared. "Perris has hopped out. Wise gent, at that. He seen the game was too big for him. And I don't blame him for quitting. Ain't nothing here that he'd come after. Them boots are wore out. The blankets and the cooking things he got from the ranch. Look at the way the blankets are piled up. Shows he quit in a rush and started away. When a gent figures on coming back, he tidies things up a little when he leaves in the morning. No, boys, he's gone. Main thing to answer is: If he ain't left the valley why ain't he here in his shack now?"

"Maybe he's hunting that damn hoss?" suggested the foreman, but his voice was weak with uncertainty.

"Hunting Alcatraz after dark?" queried Little Joe.

There was no answer possible. The last glow of twilight was fading to deep night. The trees on the edge of the clearing seemed to grow taller and blacker each moment. Certainly if it were well-nigh impossible to hunt the stallion effectively in daylight it was sheer madness to hunt him at night. Every moment they waited in the cabin, the certainty that Perris had left the valley grew greater. It showed in their voices, for every man had spoken softly at first as though for fear the spirit of the inhabitant of the shack might drift near unseen and overhear. Now their words came loud, disturbing and startling Hervey in the midst of his thoughts, as he continued wandering about the cabin, lighting match after match, striving in vain to find something which would reawaken his hopes. But there was nothing of enough worth to induce Perris to return, and finally Hervey gave up.

"We'll start on," he said at length. "You boys ride along. I'll give the place another look."

As a matter of fact, he merely wished to be alone, and he was dimly pleased as they sauntered off through the trees, their voices coming more and more vaguely back to him, until the far-off rattle of hoofs began. The last he heard of them was a high-pitched laugh. It irritated Hervey. It floated back to him thin and small, like mockery. And indeed he had failed miserably. How great was his failure he could hardly estimate in a moment and he needed quiet to sum up his losses.

First of all, he had hopelessly alienated the girl and while offending her he had failed to serve the rancher. For Red Jim Perris, driven by force from the ranch, would surely return again to exact payment in full for the treatment he had received. The whole affair was a hopeless muddle. He had staked everything on his ability to trap Perris and destroy him, thereby piling upon the shoulders of Oliver Jordan a burden of gratitude which the rancher could never repay. But now that Perris was footloose he became a danger imperilling not only Jordan but Hervey himself. The trap had closed and closed on nothing. The future presented to Hervey stark ruin.

So enthralling was the gloom of these thoughts that the foreman did not hear the thudding hoofs of a horse which trotted up through the trees. Not until horse and rider appeared in the clearing was Hervey roused and then in the first glance by the size and the tossing head of the approaching pony, he recognized the horse of Red Perris!

CHAPTER XXI
THE BATTLE

HE had time to burst from the hut and race across the clearing through the darkness which would surely shelter him from the snap-shot of even such an expert as Red Jim, but in mind and body Hervey was too paralyzed by the appearance of his enemy to stir until he saw Perris slip from his horse, slumping to the earth after the fashion of a weary man, and drag off the saddle. He paid no attention to tethering his pony, but started towards the shack, down-headed, heavy of foot.

Hervey had gained the door of the shack in the interim, and there he crouched at watch, terrified at the thought of staying till the other entered, still more terrified at the idea of bolting across the open clearing. He could see Perris clearly, in outline, for just behind him there was a rift in the circle of trees which fenced the clearing and Red Jim was thrown into somewhat bold relief against the blue-black of the night sky far beyond. He could even make out that a bandage circled the head of Perris and with that sight a new thought leaped into the brain of the foreman. The bandage, the stumbling walk, the downward head, were all signs of a badly injured and exhausted man. Suppose he were to attack Perris, single-handed and destroy him? The entire problem would be solved! The respect of his men, the deathless gratitude of Jordan were in the grip of his hand.

His fingers locked around the butt of his gun and yet he hesitated to draw. One could never be sure. How fast, how lightning fast his mind plunged through thought after thought, image after flocking image, while Red Jim made the last dragging steps towards the door of the shack! If he drew, Perris, despite his bent head might catch the glimmer of steel and draw and fire at the glance of the gun. There were tales of gun experts doing more remarkable feats. Wild Bill, in his prime, from the corner of his eye saw a man draw a white hankerchief, thought it a gun, whirled on his heel, and killed a harmless stranger.

He who stops to think can rarely act. It was true of Hervey. Then Perris, at the very door of the hut, dropped the flopping saddle to the ground and the foreman saw that no holster swung at the hip of his man. Joy leaped in him. There was no thought for the cruel cowardice of his act but only overmastering gratitude that the enemy should be thus delivered helpless into his hand. Through the split part of a second that thrill passed tingling through and through him, then he shouted: "Perris!" and at the same instant whipped out the gun and fired pointblank.

A snake will rattle before it strikes and a dog will snarl before it bares its teeth: instinct forced Hervey to that exulting cry and even as the gun came into his hand he saw Perris spin sideways. He fired and the figure at the door lunged down at him. The shoulder struck Hervey in the upturned face and smashed him backwards so that his hand flew out to break the force of the fall, knocked on the floor, and the revolver shot from the unnerved fingers.

If he had any hope that his bullet had gone home and that this was the fall of a dying man, it was instantly removed. Lean arms, amazingly swift, amazingly strong, coiled round him. Hands gripped at him with a clutch so powerful that the fingers burned into his flesh. And, most horrible of all, Red Jim fought in utter silence, as a bull-terrier fights when it goes for the throat.

The impetus of that unexpected attack, half-stunned Lew Hervey. Then the spur of terror gave him hysterical strength.

A hand caught at his throat and got a choking hold. He whirled his heavy body with all his might, tore lose, and broke to his feet. Staggering back to the wall, he saw Red Perris crouch in the door and then spring in again. Hervey struck out with all his might but felt the blow glance and then the coiling arms were around him again. Once again, in the crashing fall to the floor, the hold of Perris was broken and Hervey leaped away for the door yelling: "Perris—it's a mistake—for God's sake——"

The catlike body sprang out of the corner into which it had been flung by Hervey as the foreman rose from the floor. As well attempt to elude a panther by flight! Lew whirled with a sobbing breath of despair and smashed out again with clubbed fist. But the lithe shadow swerved as a leaf whirls from a beating hand and again their bodies crashed together.

But was it a dream that there was less power in the arms of Perris now? Had the foreman seen Red Jim lying prostrate and senseless after his battle with Alcatraz on that day, he would have understood this sudden failing of energy, but as it was he dared not trust his senses. He only knew that it was possible to tear the twining grip away, to spring back till he crashed against the side of the shanty, still pleading in a fear-maddened voice: "Perris, d'you hear? I didn't mean—"

As well appeal to a thunder-bolt. The shadowy form came again but now, surely, it was less swift and resistless. He was able to leap from the path but in dodging his legs entangled in a chair and he tumbled headlong. It was well for Hervey then that his panic was not blind, but with the surety that the end was come he whirled to his knees with the chair which had felled him gripped in both hands and straight at the lunging Perris he hurled it with all his strength. The missile went home with a crash and Red Jim slumped into a formless shadow on the floor.

Only now that a chance for flight was open to him did the strength of Hervey desert him. A nightmare weakness was in his knees so that he could hardly reel to his feet and he moved with outstretched hands towards the door until his toe clicked against his fallen revolver. He paused to scoop it up and turning back through the door, he realized suddenly that Red Jim had not moved. The body lay spilled out where it had fallen, strangely flat, strangely still.

With stumbling fingers, the foreman lighted a match and by that wobbling light he saw Perris lying on his face with his arms thrown out, as a man lies when he is knocked senseless—as a man lies when he is struck dead! Yet Hervey stood drinking in the sight until his match burned his fingers.

The old nightmare fear descended on him the moment the darkness closed about him again. He seemed to see the limp form collect itself and prepare to rise. But he fought this fancy away. He would stay and make light enough to examine the extent of his victory.

He remembered having seen paper and wood lying beside the stove. Now he scooped it up, threw off the covers of the stove, and in a moment white smoke was pouring up from the paper, then flickering bursts of flame every one of which made the body of Perris seem shuddering back to life. But presently the fire rose and Hervey could clearly see the cabin, sadly wrecked by the struggle, and the figure of Perris still moveless.

Even now he went with gingerly steps, the gun thrust out before him. It seemed a miracle that this tigerish fighter should have been suddenly reduced to the helplessness of a child. Holding the gun ready, he slipped his left hand under the fallen man and after a moment, faintly but unmistakably, he felt the beating of the heart. Let it be ended, then!

He pressed the muzzle of the revolver into the back of Perris but his finger refused to tighten around the trigger. No, the powder-burn would prove he had shot his man from behind, and that meant hanging. A tug of his left hand flopped the limp body over, but then his hands were more effectually tied than ever for the face of the unconscious man worked strangely on him.

"It's him now," thought Hervey, "or me later on."

But still he could not shoot. "Helpless as a child"—why had that comparison entered his mind? He studied the features, very pale beneath the bloody bandage which Perris had improvised when he recovered from his battle with the stallion. He was very young—terribly young. Hervey was unnerved. But suppose he let Perris come back to his senses, wakened those insolent blue eyes, started that sharp tongue to life—then it would be a very much easier matter to shoot.

So Lew went to the door, took the rope from Red Jim's saddle, and with it bound the arms of Perris to his side. Then he lifted the hanging body—how light a weight it was!—and placed it in a chair, where it doubled over, limp as a loosely stuffed scarecrow. Hervey tossed more wood on the fire and when he turned again, Perris was showing the first signs of returning consciousness, a twitching of his fingers.

After that his senses returned with astonishing speed. In the space of a moment or two he had straightened in the chair, opened dead eyes, groaned faintly, and then tugged against his bonds. It seemed that that biting of the rope into his arm-muscles cleared his mind. All in an instant he was staring straight into the eyes and into the thoughts of Hervey with full understanding.

"I see," said Perris, "it was the chair that turned the trick. You're lucky, Hervey."

It seemed to Hervey a wonderful thing that the red-headed man could be so quiet about it, and most wonderful of all that Perris could look at anything in the world rather than the big Colt which hung in the hand of the victor. And then, realizing that it was his own comparative cowardice that made this seem strange, the foreman gritted his teeth. Shame softens the heart sometimes, but more often it hardens the spirit. It hardened the conqueror against his victim, now, and made it possible for him to look down on Red Jim with a cruel satisfaction.

"Well?" he said, and the volume of his voice added to this determination.

"Well?" said Perris, as calm as ever. "Waiting for me to whine?"

Hervey blinked.

"Who licked you?" he asked, forced to change his thoughts. "Who licked you—before I got at you?"

Perris smiled, and there was something about the smile that made Hervey flush to the roots of his grey hair.

"Alcatraz had the first innings," said Perris. "He cleaned me up. And that, Hervey, was tolerably lucky for you."

"Was it?" sneered the victor. "You'd of done me up quick, maybe, if Alcatraz hadn't wore you out?"

He waited hungrily for a reply that might give him some basis on which to act, for after all, it was not going to be easy to fire pointblank into those steady, steady eyes. And more than all, he hungered to see some wavering of courage, some blenching from the thing to come.

"Done you up?" echoed Red Jim. And he ran his glance slowly, thoughtfully over the body of the foreman. "I'd of busted you in two, Hervey."

A little chilly shiver ran through Hervey but he managed to shrug the feeling away—the feeling that someone was standing behind him, listening, and looking into his shameful soul. But no one could be near. It would be simple, perfectly simple. What person in the world could doubt his story of how he met Perris at the shack and warned him again to leave the Valley of the Eagles and of how Perris went for the gun but was beaten in fair fight? Who could doubt it? An immense sense of security settled around him.

"Well," he said, "second guessing is easy, even for a fool."

"Right," nodded Red Jim. "I should of knifed you when I had you down."

"If you'd had a knife," said Hervey.

"Look at my belt, Lew."

There it was, the stout handle of a hunting knife. The same chill swept through Hervey a second time and, for a moment, he wavered in his determination. Then, with all his heart, he envied that indefinable thing in the eyes of Perris, the thing which he had hated all his life. Some horses had it, creatures with high heads, and always he had made it a point to take that proud gleam out.

"A hoss is made for work, not foolishness," he used to say.

Here it was, looking out at him from the eyes of his victim. He hated it, he feared and envied it, and from the very bottom of his heart he yearned to destroy it before he destroyed Perris.

"You know," he said with sudden savagery, "what's coming?"

"I'm a pretty good guesser," nodded Red Jim. "When a fellow tries to shoot me in the dark, and then slugs me with a chair and ties me up, I generally make it out that he figures on murder, Hervey."

He gave just the slightest emphasis to the important word, and yet something in Hervey grew tense. Murder it was, and of the most dastardly order, no matter how he tried to excuse it by protesting to himself his devotion to Oliver Jordan. The lies we tell to our own souls about ourselves are the most damning ones, as they are also the easiest. But Hervey found himself so cornered that he dared not think about his act. He stopped thinking, therefore, and began to shout. This is logical and human, as every woman knows who has found an irate husband in the wrong. Hervey began to hate with redoubled intensity the man he was about to destroy.

"You come here and try to play the cock of the walk," cried the foreman. "It don't work. You try to face me out before all my men. You threaten me. You show off your gun-fighting, damn you, and then you call it murder when I beat you fair and square and—"

He found it impossible to continue. The prisoner was actually smiling.

"Hound dogs always hunt in the dark," said Red Jim.

A quiver of fear ran through Hervey. Indeed, he was haunted by chilly uneasiness all the time. In vain he assured himself with reason that his victim was utterly helpless. A ghostly dread remained in the back of his mind that through some mysterious agency the red-headed man would be liberated, and then——. Hervey shuddered in vital earnest. What would happen to a crow that dared trap an eagle.

"I'm due back at the ranch," said Hervey, "to tell 'em how you jumped me here while I was waiting here quiet to warn you again to get out of the Valley of the Eagles peaceable. Before I go, Perris, is they anything you want done, any messages you want to leave behind you?"

And he set his teeth when he saw that Perris did not blench. He was perfectly quiet. Nearness to death sometimes acts in this manner. It reduces men to the unaffected simplicity of children.

"No message, thanks," said Red Jim. "Nobody to leave them to and nothing to leave but a hoss that somebody else will ride and a gun that somebody else will shoot."

"And the girl?" said Lew Hervey.

And a thrill of consummate satisfaction passed through him, for Red Perris had plainly been startled out of his calm.

"A girl?"

"You know what I mean. Marianne Jordan."

He smiled knowingly.

"Well?" said Perris, breathing hard.

"Why, you fool," cried the foreman, "don't you know she's gone plumb wild about you? Didn't she come begging to me to get you out of trouble?"

"You lie!" burst out Perris.

But by his roving glance, by the sudden outpouring of sweat which gleamed on his forehead, Hervey knew that he had shaken his man to the soul. By playing carefully on this string might he not reduce even this care-free fighter to trembling love of life? Might he not make Red Perris cringe! All cowards feel that their own vice exists in others. Hervey, in his entire life, had dreaded nothing saving Red Jim, and now he felt that he had found the thing which would make life too dear to Perris to be given up with a smile.

"Begging? I'll tell a man she did!" nodded Hervey.

"It's because she's plumb generous. She thought that might turn you. Why—she don't hardly know me!"

"Don't she?" sneered Hervey. "You don't figure her right. She's one of the hit or miss kind. She hated me the minute she laid eyes on me—hated me for nothing! And you knocked her off her feet the first shot. That's all there is to it. She'd give the Valley of the Eagles for a smile from you."

He saw the glance of Perris wander into thin distance and soften. Then the eye of Red Jim returned to his tormentor, desperately. The blow had told better than Hervey could have hoped.

"And me a plain tramp—a loafer—me!" said Perris to himself. He added suddenly: "Hervey, let's talk man to man!"

"Go on," said the foreman, and set his teeth to keep his exultation from showing.

Five minutes more, he felt, and Perris would be begging like a coward for his life.

CHAPTER XXII
MCGUIRE SLEEPS

NEVER did a fox approach a lion with more discretion than Marianne approached the careless figure of McGuire. His very attitude was a warning that her task was to be made as difficult as possible. He had pushed his sombrero, limp with age and wear, far back on his head, and now, gazing, apparently, into the distant blue depths of the sky, he regarded vacancy with mild interest and blew in the same direction a thin brownish vapor of smoke. Obviously he expected an argument; he was leading her on. And just as obviously he wanted the argument merely for the sake of killing time. He was in tremendous need of amusement. That was all.

She wanted to go straight to him with a bitter appeal to his manhood, to his mercy as a man. But she realized that this would not do at all. A strenuous attack would simply rouse him. Therefore she called up from some mysterious corner of her tormented heart a smile, or something that would do duty as a smile. Strangely enough, no sooner had the smile come than her whole mental viewpoint changed. It became easy to make the smile real; half of her anxiety fell away. And dropping one hand on her hip, she said cheerfully to McGuire.

"You look queer as a prison-guard, Mr. McGuire."

She made a great resolve, that moment, that if she were ever safely through the catastrophe which now loomed ahead, she would diminish the distance between her and her men and form the habit of calling them by their first names. She could not change as abruptly in a moment, but she understood perfectly, that if she had been able to call McGuire by some foolish and familiar nickname, half of his strangeness would immediately melt away. As it was, she made the best of a bad matter by throwing all the gentle good nature possible into her voice, and she was rewarded by seeing McGuire jerk up his head and jerk down his glance at her. At the same time, he crimsoned to the eyes, changing his weathered complexion to a flaring, reddish-brown.

"Prison-guard?" said McGuire. "Me?"

"Well," answered Marianne, "that's the truth, isn't it? You're the guard and I'm the prisoner?"

"I'm watching these hosses," said McGuire. "That's all. They ain't no money could hire me to guard a woman."

"Really?" said Marianne.

"Sure. I used to have a wife. I know."

She laughed, a little hysterically, but McGuire treated the mirth as a compliment to his jest and joined in with a tremendous guffaw. His eyes were still wet with mirth as she said: "Too bad you have to waste time like this, with such a fine warm day for sleeping. Couldn't you trust the corral bars to take care of the horses?"

His glance twinkled with understanding. It was plain that he appreciated her point and the way she made it.

"Them hosses are feeling their oats," said McGuire. "Can't tell what they'd be up to the minute I turned my back on 'em. Might jump that old fence and be off, for all I know."

"Well," said Marianne, "they look quite contented. And if one of them did take advantage of you and run away while you slept, I'm sure it would come home again."

He had quite fallen into the spirit of the thing.

"Maybe," grinned McGuire, "but I might wake up out of a job."

"Well," said Marianne, "there have been times when I would have weighed one hour of good sleep against two jobs as pleasant as this. How much real damage might that sleep do?"

"If it took me out of the job? Oh, I dunno. Might take another month before I landed a place as good."

"Surely not as long as that. But isn't it possible that your sleep might be worth *two* months' wages to you, Mr. McGuire?"

"H-m-m," growled McGuire, and his little shifty eyes fastened keenly on her. "You sure mean business!"

"As much as anyone in the world could!" cried the girl, suddenly serious.

And for a moment they stared at each other.

"Lady," said McGuire at length, "I begin to feel sort of yawny and sleepy, like."

"Then sleep," said Marianne, her voice trembling in spite of herself. "You might have pleasant dreams, you know—of a murder prevented—of a man's life saved!"

McGuire jerked his sombrero low over his eyes.

"You think it's as bad as that?" he growled, glaring at her.

"I swear it is!"

He considered another moment. Then: "You'll have to excuse me, Miss Jordan. But I'm so plumb tired out I can't hold up my end of this talk no longer!"

So saying, he dropped his head on both his doubled fists, and she lost sight of his face. It had come so inconceivably easily, this triumph, that she was too dazed to move, for a moment. Then she turned and fairly raced for the corral. It had all been the result of the first smile with which she went to McGuire, she felt. And as she saddled her bay in a shed a moment later she was blessing the power of laughter. It had given her the horse. It had let her pass through the bars. It placed her on the open road where she fled away at a swift gallop, only looking back, as she reached the top of the first hill, to see McGuire still seated on the stump, but now his head was canted far to one side, and she had no doubt that he must be asleep in very fact.

Then the hill rose behind her, shutting out the ranch, and she turned to settle to her work. Never in her life—and she had ridden cross-country on blood horses in the East—had she ridden as she rode on this day! She was striking on a straight line over hill and dale, through the midst of barbed wire. But the wire halted her only for short checks. The swift snipping of the pair of pliers which was ever in her saddle bag cleared the way, and as the lengths of wire snapped humming back, coiling like snakes, she rode through and headed into the next field at a renewed gallop. She was leaving behind her a day's work for half a dozen men, but she would have sacrificed ten times the value of the whole ranch to gain another half hour of precious time.

For when she broke down the last of the small fenced fields the sun was already down. And when twilight came, she knew by instinct, the blow would fall. Yet the distance to the shack was still terribly far.

She straightened the gallant little bay to her work, but at every stride she moaned. Oh for such legs beneath her as the legs of Lady Mary, stretching swiftly and easily over the ground! But this chopping, laboring stride—! She struck her hand against her forehead and then spurred mercilessly. As a result, the bay merely tossed her head, for she was already drawn straight as a string by the effort of her gallop. And Marianne had to sit back in the saddle and simply pray for time, while the little thirty-two revolver in the saddle holster before her, flapped monotonously, beating out the rhythm of every stride.

And the night rode over the mountains with mysterious speed. It seemed to her frantic brain that the gap between crimson sunset and pallid twilight could have been spanned by a scant five minutes. And now, when she found herself at the foot of the last slope, it was the utter dark, and above her head the white stars were rushing past the treetops. The slope was killing the mare. She fell from her labored gallop to a trot, from the trot to a shambling jog, and then to a walk. And all the time Marianne found herself listening with desperate intensity for the report of a gun out of the woods ahead!

She threw herself out of the saddle, cast hardly a glance at the drooping figure of the bay, and ran forward on foot, stumbling in the dark over fallen branches, slipping more than once and dropping flat on her face as her feet shot back without foothold from the pine needles. But she picked herself up again and flung herself at her work with a frantic determination.

Through the trees, filtered by the branches, she saw a light. But when she came to the edge of the clearing she made out that the illumination came from a fire, not a lantern. The interior of the cabin was awash with shadows, and across the open doorway of the hut the monstrous and obscure outline of a standing man wavered to and fro. There was no clamor of many voices. And her heart leaped with relief. Hervey and his men, then, had lost heart at the last moment. They had not dared to attack Red Jim Perris in spite of their numbers!

But her joy died, literally, mid-leap.

"Hervey," cried the voice of Perris, a trembling and fear-sharpened voice, "for God's sake, wait!"

Red Perris begging, cringing to any man, to Lew Hervey? All at once she went weak and sick, but she hurried straight towards the cabin, trying to cry out. Her throat was closed. She could not utter so much as a whisper.

"Listen to me!" went on Perris. "I've been a fool all my life. I know it now. I've wandered around fighting and playing like a block-head. I've wanted nothing but action and I've got it. But now you tell me that I've had something else right in the hollow of my hand and I didn't know it! Maybe you've lied about her. I dunno. But just the thought that she might care a little about me has——"

Marianne stopped short in the darkness and a hot wave of shame blotted out the rest of the words until the heavier voice of the foreman began again.

"Maybe you'd have me think you're kind of fond of the girl—that you love her, all at once, just because I told you she's in love with you?"

"I'd have you think it and I'd have you believe it. When a gent sits looking into the face of a gun he does his thinking and his living mighty fast and condensed. And I know this, that if you turn me loose alive, Hervey, I'll give you my word that I'll forget what's happened. You think I'll hit your trail with a gat. But you're wrong. Make your own bargain, partner. But when I think of what life might be now—Hervey, I can't die now! I'm not ready to die!"

She had been stumbling in a daze towards the door. Now she came suddenly in view of them, the broad back of Hervey turned towards her and Perris facing her, his face white, drawn, and changed. And the blood-stained bandage about his forehead. He leaned forward in his chair in the fervor of his appeal, his arms lashed against his sides with the loose of a lariat.

"Are you through begging?" sneered Hervey.

It threw Perris back in the chair like a blow in the face. Then he straightened.

"You've told me all this just to see me weaken, eh, Hervey?"

"And I've seen it," said Hervey. "I've seen you ready to take water. That's all I wanted. You've lost your grip and you'll never get it back. Right now you're all hollow inside. Perris, you can't look me in the eye!"

"You lie," said Red Jim quietly, and lifting his head, he stared full into the face of his tormentor. "You made a hound out of me, but only for a minute, Hervey."

And then she saw him stiffen in the chair, and his eyes narrow. The chains of fear and of shame which had bound her snapped.

"Hervey!" she cried, and as he whirled she came panting into the door.

Just for an instant she saw a devil glitter in his eyes but in a moment his glance wavered. He admitted himself beaten as he thrust his revolver into the holster.

"Talk wouldn't make Perris leave," he mumbled. "I been trying to throw a little scare into him. And the bluff would of worked if—"

She cut in on him: "I heard enough to understand. I know what you tried to do. Oh, Lew Hervey, if this could be told, your own men would run you down like a mad dog!"

He had grown livid with a mixture of emotions.

"If it could be told. Maybe. But it can't be told! Keep clear of him, or I'll drill him, by God!" She obeyed, stepping back from Jim.

He backed towards the door where the saddle of Perris lay, and stooping, he snatched the revolver of Red Jim from the saddle-holster. For the moment, at least, his enemy was disarmed and there was no fear of immediate pursuit.

"I still have a day or two," he said. "And the game ain't ended. Remember that, Perris. It ain't ended till Jordan comes back."

And he turned into the darkness which closed over him at once like the falling of a blanket.

"You won't follow him?" she pleaded.

He shook his head and a moment later, under the touch of his own hunting knife which she drew, the rope parted and freed his arms. At the same instant she heard the hoofs of Hervey's horse crashing through the underbrush down the mountain side. And not till that final signal of success reached her did Marianne give way to the hysteria which had been flooding higher and higher in her throat ever since those words of Hervey had arrested her in the clearing. But once released it came in a rush, blinding her, so that she could not see Perris through her tears as he placed her gently in the chair. Only through the wild confusion of her sobbing she could hear his voice saying words she did not understand, over and over again, but she knew that his voice was infinitely soft, infinitely reassuring.

Then her mind cleared and her nerves steadied with amazing suddenness, just as the wind at a stroke will tumble the storm clouds aside and leave a placid blue sky above. She found Red Jim kneeling beside the chair with his arms around her and her head on his shoulder, wet with her tears. For the first time she could hear and really understand what he had been saying over and over again. He was telling her that he loved her, would always love her, that he could forgive Lew Hervey, even, because of the message which he had brought.

Had she confessed everything, then, in the hysteria? Had she confirmed what Lew Hervey said? Yes, for the voice of Red Jim was unquestioning, cherishing as men will the thing which they love and own.

"You're better now?" he asked at length.

"Yes," she answered, "I'm weak—and ashamed—and—what have I said to you?"

"Something that's made me happier than a king. And I'll make it a thing you'll never have to regret, so help me God!"

He raised her to her feet.

"Now you have to go home—at once."

"And you?"

"Hervey will come hunting me again tomorrow, and he'll have his men with him. He doesn't know I've forgotten him. He thinks it's his life or mine, and he'll try to run me down."

"The sheriff—" she cried fiercely.

"That's where I'm going. To Glosterville to hide like a coward where the sheriff can look out for me. I can't take chances now. I don't belong to myself. When your father comes back and takes charge of the ranch, and Hervey, I'll come when you send for me. I'll get my things together to-night, ride down the valley so they can't trap me again here, camp out for an hour or so in the morning, and then cut out across the Eagles. But you're strong enough to ride home?"

She nodded, and they walked side by side out across the clearing and down towards the place where she had left the bay. And it seemed to Marianne, leaning a little on the arm of Red Jim, that she had shifted the whole burden of her worries onto the shoulders of her lover. Her troubles disappeared. The very sound of his voice assured her of happiness forever.

They found the bay. The tough little mustang was already much recuperated, and Perris swept Marianne into the saddle. She leaned to kiss him. In the dark her lips touched the bandage around his head.

"It's where Hervey struck you down!" she exclaimed. "Jim, you can't ride across the mountains so terribly hurt—"

"It's only a scratch," he assured her. "I met Alcatraz to-day, and he won again! But the third time—"

Marianne shivered.

"Don't speak of him! He haunts me, Jim. The very mention of him takes all the happiness out of me. I feel—almost as if there were a bad fate in him. But you promise, that you won't stay to take one final chance? You won't linger in the Valley to hunt Alcatraz again? You'll ride straight across the mountains when the morning comes?"

"I promise," answered Perris.

But afterwards, as he watched her drift away through the darkness calling back to him from time to time until her voice dwindled to a bird-note and then faded away, Red Jim prayed in his heart of hearts that he would not chance upon sight of the stallion in the morning, for if he did, he knew that the first solemn promise of his life would be broken.

CHAPTER XXIII
LOBO

THE dawn of the next day came cold and grey about Alcatraz, grey because the sheeted clouds that promised a storm were covering the sky, and cold with a wind out of the north. When he lifted his head, he saw where the first rains had covered the slopes of the Eagle Mountains with tenderest green, and looking higher, the snows were gathering on the summits. The prophetic thickening of his coat foretold a hard winter.

Now he was on watch with the mares in the hollow behind and himself on the crest rarely turning his head from a wisp of smoke which rose far south. He knew what that meant. Red Perris was on his trail again, and this was the morning-fire of the Great Enemy. He had lain on the ground like a dead man the day before. Now he was risen to battle again! Instinctively he swung his head and looked at the place where the saddle had rested the day before, the saddle which he had worked off with so much wild rolling and scraping against rocks.

He nibbled the grass as he watched, or now and again jerked up his head to catch the scents which blow truer in the upper air-currents.

It was on one of these occasions that he caught an odor only vaguely known to him, and known as a danger. He had never been able to label it but he knew that when the grey mare caught such a scent she was even more perturbed than when man rode into view. So now he breathed deep, his great eyes shining with excitement. What could this danger be which was more to be dreaded than the Great Enemy? Yielding to curiosity, he headed straight up wind to make sure.

No doubt he thereby gave proof that he was unfitted to lead wild horses in the mountains. The wise black of former days, or the grey mare now, would never have stopped to question, but gathering the herd with the alarm call, they would have busied themselves with unrolling mile after mile behind their flying heels. Alcatraz increased his walk to a trot, promptly lost the scent altogether, and headed onto the next elevation to see if he could catch it again. He stood there for a long moment, raising and lowering his head, and then turning a little sidewise so that the wind would cut into his nostrils—which was a trick the grey had taught him. The scent was gone and the wind blew to him only the pure coolness of dew, just sharpened to fragrance by a scent of distant sagebrush. He gave up and turned about to head for the mares.

The step for which he raised his forefoot was not completed for down the hollow behind him he saw a grey skulker slinking with its belly close to the ground. If it stood erect it would be as tall as a calf new-born. The tail was fluffy, the coat of fur a veritable mane around the throat, the head long of muzzle and broad across the forehead with dark marks between the eyes and arching like brows above them so that the facial expression was one of almost human wisdom and wistfulness. It was a beautiful creature to watch, as its smooth trot carried it with incredible speed across the stallion's line of retreat, but Alcatraz had seen those grey kings of the mountains before and knew everything about them except their scent. He saw no beauty in the lofer wolf.

The blood which congealed in his veins was released; he reared and wheeled and burst away at full gallop; there was a sobbing whine of eagerness behind him—the lobo was stretched in pursuit.

Never in his life had the chestnut run as he ran now, and never had he fled so hopelessly. He knew that one slash of those great white teeth would cut his throat to the vital arteries. He knew that for all his speed he had neither the foot nor the wind to escape the grey marauder. It was only a matter of time, and short time at that, before the end came. The lofer prefers young meat and as a rule will cut down a yearling colt, or dine on warm veal, eschewing cold flesh and feeding only once from every kill—the lobo being the Lucullus of beasts of prey—but this prowler had either found scanty fare in a long journey across the mountains or else he wished to kill now for pure deviltry and not from hunger. At any rate, he slid over the ground like the shadow of a cloud driven in a storm.

Already he gained fast, and yet he had not attained top speed; when he did, he would walk up on the chestnut as the latter could walk up on the mares of his herd.

Over a hill bolted Alcatraz and beneath him he saw a faint hope of escape—the flash of water where a brook, new-swelled by the rains, was running bankfull, a noisy torrent. He went down the slope like the wind, struck the level at such speed that the air stung his nostrils, and leaped from the firm gravel at the edge of the stream.

The far bank seemed a mighty distance as he soared high—the water rushed broad and swift beneath him, no swimming if he struck that bubbling current—and then, a last pitch forwards in mid-air; a forefoot struck ground, the bank crushed in beneath his weight, and then he was scrambling to the safety beyond and reeling into a new gallop.

Behind him, he saw the shadowy pursuer skim down the slope, fling into the air, and drop out of sight. Had he reached the shore? Ten seconds—no long and ominous head appeared—certainly he had fallen short and landed in the furious current. Alcatraz dropped his heart-breaking pace to a moderate gallop, but as he did so he saw a form which dripped with water scramble into view fifty yards down-stream—the lobo had managed to reach safety after all and now he came like a bullet to end the chase.

There was only half a hope left to Alcatraz and that was to turn and attempt to leave the wolf again at the water-jump; but now his renewed panic paralyzed all power of thinking. He did not even do the next best thing—race straight away in a true line, but bearing off first to the left and then to the right, he shot across the hills in a miserably wavering flight.

The lobo came like doom behind him. The chill of the water had enraged him. Besides, he did not often have to waste such time and energy to make a kill, and now, bent on a quick ending, the fur which fringed his lean belly cut the dew from the grass as he stretched to his full and matchless speed. Alcatraz saw and strained forward but he had reached his limit and the wolf gained with the passage of every second.

Another danger appeared. Off to the side and well ahead, spurring his mount to top effort, came Red Perris, who must have marked the chase with his glass. Alcatraz gave him not a glance, not a thought. What was the whisper and burn of a rope, what was even the hum of a bullet compared with the tearing teeth of the lofer wolf? So he kept to his course, stretched straight from the tip of his nose to the end of his flying tail and marking from the corner of his eye that the lobo still gained vital inches at every leap.

The horseman to his left shot over a hill and disappeared into the hollow beyond—he would be a scant hundred yards away when Alcatraz raced by, if indeed he could keep beyond reach of the wolf as long as this. And that was more than doubtful—impossible! For the grey streak had shot from behind until it now was at his tail, at his flank, with red tongue lolling and the sound of its panting audible. Half a minute more and it would be in front and heading him, and when he whirled the creature would spring.

And so it happened. The killer swept to the front and snapped—at the flash of the teeth Alcatraz wheeled, saw the monster leave the ground—and then a limp weight struck his shoulder and rolled heavily back to the ground; but not until he had straightened away on his new course did Alcatraz hear the report of the rifle, so much had the bullet outdistanced the sound.

He looked back.

Red Perris sat in his saddle with the rifle coming slowly down from his shoulder. The lofer wolf lay with a smear of red across one side of his head. Then a hill rose behind the stallion and shut off his view.

He brought down his gait to a stumbling canter for now a great weakness was pouring through his legs and his heart fluttered and trembled like the heart of a yearling when it first feels the strain and burn of the rope. He was saved, but by how small a margin! He was saved, but in his mind grew another problem. Why had the Great Enemy chosen to kill the wolf and spare the horse? And how great was his greatness who could strike down from afar that king of flesh-eaters in the very moment of a kill! But he knew, very clearly, that he had been in the hollow of the man's hand and had been spared; and that he had been rescued from certain death; was not the scent of the wolf's pelt still in his nostrils as the creature had leaped?

He came to the brook and snorted in wonder. In a sane moment he would never have attempted that leap. For that matter, perhaps, no other horse between the seas would have ever dreamed of the effort. Alcatraz headed up the stream for a narrow place, shaking his head at the roar of the current.

CHAPTER XXIV
THE CRISIS

WHEN he found a place where he could jump the Little Smoky he picked up his mares again and led them straight north, accepting their whinnies of congratulation with a careless toss of his head as though only women-folk would bother to think of such small matters. He had a definite purpose, now. He had had enough of the Valley of the Eagles with its haunting lobos and its cunning human hunters. And he chose for exit the cañon of the Little Smoky itself. For there were many blind ravines pocketing the sides of the Valley of the Eagles, but the little Smoky would lead him straight to the summits. He looked back as he reached the mouth of the gorge, filled with the murmur of the rain-swollen waters. Perris was drifting towards them. And Alcatraz tossed his head and struck into a canter.

It was a precaution which he never abandoned, for while the Great Enemy was most to be feared, there were other human foes and such a narrow-throated gorge as this would ideally serve them as a trap. He shortened his lope so as to be ready to whirl away as he came to the first winding between the rugged walls of the valley—but the ground was clear before him and calling up his lagging herd, he made on towards a sound of falling water ahead. It was a new sound to Alcatraz in that place, for he remembered no cataract in this gorge. But every water-course had been greatly changed since the rains began, and who could tell what alterations had occurred here?

Who, indeed, could have guessed it? For as he swung about the next bend he was confronted by a sheer wall of rock over which the falling torrent of the Little Smoky was churned to white spray by projecting fragments. Far above, the side of the mountain was still marked by a raw wound where the landslide had swept, cutting deeper and deeper, until it choked the narrow ravine with an incalculable mass of sand, crushed trees, and a rubble of broken stone. It had dammed the Little Smoky, but soon topping the obstruction, the river now poured over the crest and filled the valley with a noise of rushing and shouting so caught up by echoes that Alcatraz seemed to be standing inside a whole circle of invisible waterfalls.

He wondered at that sight for only an instant; then, as the meaning drove home to him, he wheeled and raced down the valley. This was the explanation of the Enemy's move towards the throat of the cañon!

He passed the mares like a red streak of light, his ears flagging back and his tail swept out straight behind by the wind of his gallop. He rushed about the next turn of the cliff and saw that the race had been in vain—the Great Enemy was spurring his reeling cowpony into the mouth of the Little Smoky gap!

The chestnut made his calculations without slackening his pace. The man was in the valley, but he had not yet reached that narrow throat where his lariat was of sufficient radius to cover the space between the wall of the cañon and the stream. However, he was in excellent position to maneuver for a throw in case Alcatraz tried to slip by. Therefore he now brought his pony to a slow lope, and loosening his rope, he swung the noose in a wide circle; he was ready to plunge to either side and cast the lariat.

Being nearer to the river than to the cañon wall it was in the latter direction that the stallion found the wider free space and towards it, accordingly, he directed his flight, running as he had only run when the lofer wolf dogged his heels. It was only a feint. His eye was too keen in the calculation of distances and relative speeds not to realize that the cowpony would beat him to the goal, yet he kept up his furious pace even when Perris had checked his horse to a trot. Straight on swept Alcatraz until he saw the glitter of the hunter's eyes beneath the wide brim of his sombrero—then he braced his legs, knocking up a small shower of sand and rocks, swerved to the left, and bolted for the river bank.

Even as he made the move, though blinded by the fierceness of his own effort, he knew that it would be a tight squeeze. Had the pony under Perris possessed half of its ordinary speed of foot it would easily have headed the fugitive or at the least brought its rider in rope-throw, now, outworn by the long trail it had followed, the little animal stumbled and almost fell when Perris with iron hand swung it around. That blunder lost fatal yards, but still it did its honest best. It was a veteran of many a round-up. No pony in the arduous work of cutting out was surer of eye or quicker of foot, and now this dodging back and forth brought a gleam into the bronco's eyes. There was no need of the goading spur of Perris to make it spring forth at full speed, running on nerve-power in place of the sapped strength of muscle.

The stumble had given Alcatraz a fighting chance for his freedom—that was all. He recognized the flying peril as he raced in a wide loping semicircle. If the river were twenty yards further off he, running two feet to the cowpony's one, would brush through safely, but as it was no one could tell. He knew the reach of a lariat as well as a man; had not Cordova tormented him devilishly with one time and again? Estimating the speed of his approaching enemy and the reach of the rope he felt that he could still gain freedom—unless luck was against him.

The burst of Alcatraz for the river and safety was a remarkable explosion of energy. Out of the corner of his reddening eye, as he gained swift impetus after his swerve, he saw the cowpony wheel, falter, and then burst across in pursuit to close the gap. He heeled over to the left, and found a mysterious source of energy within him that enabled his speed to be increased, until, at the top of his racing gait, he reached the very verge of the stream. There remained nothing now but a straight dash for freedom.

Luck favored him in one respect at least. The swollen current of the Little Smoky had eaten away its banks so that there was a sheer drop, straight as a cliff in most places, to the water, and the cliff-edge above was solidly compacted sand and gravel. A better race-track could hardly have been asked and the heart of Alcatraz swelled with hope as he saw the ground spin back behind him. Red Perris, too, shouting like a mad man as he spurred in, realized that his opportunity was slipping through his fingers. For now, though far away, he swung his rope in a stiffly horizontal circle about his head. The time had come. Straight before him shot the red streak of the stallion; and leaning in his saddle to give greater length to the cast he made the throw.

It failed. Even as the noose whirled above him Alcatraz knew the cast would fall short. An instant later, falling, it slapped against his shoulder and he was through the gap free! But at the contact of that dreaded lariat instinct forced him to do what reason told him was unneeded—he veered some vital inches off towards the edge of the bank.

Thereby his triumph was undone! The gravel which made so good a footing was, after all, a brittle support and now, under his pounding hoofs, the whole side of the bank gave way. A squeal of terror broke from Alcatraz. He swerved sharply in, but it was too late. The very effort to change direction brought a greater weight upon his rear hoofs and now they crushed down through flying gravel and sand. He faced straight in, pawing the yielding bank with his forehoofs and suspended over the roar of the torrent. It was like striving to climb a hill of quicksand. The greater his struggle the more swiftly the treacherous soil melted under his pounding hoofs.

Last of all, he heard a yell of horror from the Great Enemy and saw the hands of the man go up before his eyes to shut out the sight. Then Alcatraz pitched back into thin air.

He caught one glimpse of the wildly blowing storm-clouds above him, then he crashed with stinging force into the water below.

CHAPTER XXV
THE LITTLE SMOKY

PURE madness poured into the brain of Red Perris as he saw the fall. Here, then was the end of the trail, and that great battle would never be fought. Groaning he rode to the bank of the stream, mechanically gathering up the rope as he went.

He saw below him nothing but the rush of water, white riffles showing its speed. An occasional dark steak whirled past—the trunks of trees which the Little Smoky had chewed away from their foothold on its sides. Doubtless one of these burly missiles had struck and instantly killed the stallion.

But no, yonder his head broke above the surface—a great log flung past him, missing the goal by inches—a whirl in the current rolled him under,—but up he came again, swimming gallantly. The selfish rage which had consumed Red Perris broke out in words. Down the bank he trotted the buckskin, shaking his fist at Alcatraz and pouring the stream of his curses at that devoted head. Was this the reward of labor, the reward of pain and patience through all the weeks, the sleepless nights, the weary days?

"Drown, and be damned!" shouted Red Perris, and as if in answer, the body of the stallion rose miraculously from the stream and the hunter gasped his incredulity. Alcatraz was facing up stream, half his body above the surface.

The explanation was simple. At this point the Little Smoky abated its speed a little and had dropped a load of rolling stones and sand. An hour later it might be washed away, but now it made a strong bank with the current skimming above the surface. On this the stallion had struck, and whirling with the current he faced towards the source of the valley and looked into the volleying waters. Here, surely, was a sight to make a weakling tremble. But to the astonishment of Perris, he saw the head of the stallion raised, and the next moment the thunder of his neigh rang high above the voices of the river, as though he bade defiance to his destroyer, as though he called on the God of Gods to bear witness that he died without fear.

"By the Eternal!" breathed Red Perris, smitten with awe, and the next instant, the ground giving way beneath him, Alcatraz was bowled over and over, only to come up again farther down the stream.

He turned his head. Far away he made out a line of horsemen—grey, ghostly figures miles away. Hervey was keeping to his word, then. But the thought of his own danger did not hold Red Jim Perris for a moment. Down there in the thundering water Alcatraz was dying!

The heart of Red Perris went out to the dauntless chestnut. He spurred down the bank until he was even with the struggler. He swayed far out, riding the mustang so near the brink that the poor creature shuddered. He capped his hands about his lips and the hunter screamed encouragement to the hunted, yelled advice, shrieked his warnings when treetrunks hurtled from behind.

It seemed to Red Perris that Alcatraz was not a brute beast but a soul about to perish. So much do brave men love courage! Then he saw, a hundred yards away, that the bank of the stream fell away until it became a gradually shoaling beach to the water edge. With a shout of hope he raced to this point of vantage and flung himself from the saddle. Then, grasping the rope, he ran into the stream until it foamed with staggering force about his hips.

But would Alcatraz live among those sweeping treetrunks and come within casting distance of the rope? Even if he did, would the rope catch around that head of which only the nose and eyes were showing? Even if it caught could the stallion be drawn to shoal water without being strangled by the slip-knot? Had Perris been a calm man he would have discarded the thousandth chance which remained after all of these possibilities. He would have looked, instead, to his cowpony which was now cantering away towards liberty in the rear of the flying squadron of mares. But Perris saw and lived for only one thing.

Down came that brave head, but now with the ears flattened, for in the fury of the river his strength was being rapidly exhausted. Down the current it came, momentarily nearer but always with dangers shooting about it. Even while Perris looked, a great tree from which the branches had not yet been stripped rushed from behind. The hunter's yell of alarm was drowned by the thousand voices of the Little Smoky, and over that head the danger swept.

Red Perris closed his eyes and his head fell, but when he looked again the tree was far down stream and the stallion still swam in the central current, but now near, very near. Only the slender outer branches could have struck him, and these with barely sufficient force to drive him under.

Perris strode still further into the wild water until it foamed about his waist, and stretching out his arms he called to the stallion. Had he possessed ten times the power of voice he could not have made himself heard above the rioting of the Little Smoky but his gesture could be seen, and even a dumb beast could understand it. The chestnut, at least, comprehended for to the joy of Perris he now saw those gallant ears come forward again, and turning as well as he could, Alcatraz swam stoutly for the shore. In the hour of need, the Great Enemy had become his last hope.

But his progress towards the sloping bank was small. For every inch he fought to the bank the current carried him a foot down stream, yet those inches gained in the lateral direction were every one priceless. Finally Perris swung the lariat and shot it through the air. Fair and true the circle struck above the head of the stallion and the hunter shouted with hysterical triumph; a moment later he groaned as the current whirled the rope over the head of Alcatraz and down stream.

Yet he fought the hopeless fight. Staggering in the currents, beaten from his footing time and again, Perris stumbled down stream gathering his rope for a new cast as he went. Neither had the chestnut abandoned the struggle. His last efforts had swerved him about and now he headed up stream with the water foaming about his red, distended nostrils; but still through the whipping spray his great eyes were fixed on Perris. As for the man, there was a prayer in the voice with which he shouted: "Alcatraz!" and hurled the rope again.

Heavy with the water it had soaked up the noose splashed in a rough circle around the head of the swimmer and then cut down into the water. Hand over hand he drew in the slack, felt resistance, then a jar that toppled him from his foothold. The noose had indeed caught around the neck of the stallion, but the success threatened to be his ruin. Toppled head over heels in the rush of the Little Smoky, still his left hand gripped the rope and as he came gasping to the surface his feet struck and lodged strongly against the surface of a great boulder. His one stroke of luck!

He had no time to give thanks. The next moment the full weight of the torrent on Alcatraz whipped the lariat quivering out of the water. The horse was struggling in the very center of the strongest current and the tug on the arms of Perris made his shoulder sockets ache. He endured that pain, praying that his hands would not slip on the wet rope. Then, little by little, he increased his pull until all the strength of leg muscles, back, and arms was brought to bear. It seemed that there was no result; Alcatraz did not change his position; but inch by inch the rope crept in to him; he at length could shift holds, whipping his right hand in advance of the left and tugging again. There was more rapid progress, now, but as the first frenzy of nervous energy was dissipated, a tremor of exhaustion passed through his limbs and the beat of his heart redoubled until he was well-nigh stifled. True, the rope was coming in hand over hand, now, but another danger. The head of Alcatraz was sinking, his nostrils distended to the bursting point, his eyes red and bulging from their sockets. He was being throttled by the grip of the slip knot; and an instant later his head disappeared beneath the surface.

Then all weakness passed from Red Perris; there was invigorating wine in the air he breathed; a vast power clothed him suddenly and while the frenzy endured he drew Alcatraz swiftly in from the gripping currents and to the comparatively mild swirl of water where he stood. Wavering, distorted, and dim as an image in a dull mirror, he saw the form of the horse float towards him beneath the water. Still the frenzy was on him. It enabled him to spring from his place, tear the strangling noose from the neck of the stallion, and lifting that lifeless head in both hands struggle towards the shore. The water buoyed a weight which he could not otherwise have budged; he stumbled in the shoaling gravel to his knees, rose again lifting and straining, until blackness rushed across his eyes; and he pitched forward on his face.

He wakened in a whipping rain that stung the back of his neck and as he propped himself on his arms he found that he had been lying across the neck and shoulders of the stallion. That much of him, and the slender forelegs, was clear of the water. But had he not brought a dead thing to land?

He bent his cheek to the nostrils of Alcatraz, but he felt no breath. He came reeling to his knees and slid his hand beneath the water to the heart of the horse; he felt no reassuring throb. Yet he could not be sure that the end was indeed come, for the blood raged and surged through his brain and waves of violent trembling passed over him so that his sense of touch might well belie the truth. How long had he lain unconscious—a minute or an hour?

At least, he must try to get the body farther ashore. Alas, his strength hardly sufficed now to raise the head alone and when he made his effort his legs crumpled beneath him. There he sat with the head of Alcatraz in his lap—he the hunter and this the hunted!

There was small measure of religion in Red Perris but now, in helplessness, he raised his trembling hands to the stormy grey of the sky above him.

"God A'mighty," said Red Perris, "I sure ain't done much to make You listen to me, but I got this to say: that if they's a call for something to die right now it ain't the hoss that's to blame. It's me that hounded him into the river. Alcatraz ain't any pet, but he's sure lived according to his rights. Let him live and I'll let him go free. I got no right to him. I didn't make him. I never owned him. But let him stand up on his four legs again; let me see him go galloping once more, the finest hoss that ever bucked a fool man out of the saddle, and I'll call it quits!"

It was near to a prayer, if indeed this were not a prayer in truth. And glancing down to the head on his lap, he shivered with superstitious wonder. Alcatraz had unquestionably drawn a long and sighing breath.

CHAPTER XXVI
PARTNERS

THE recovery was no miracle. The strangling coil of rope which shut off the wind of Alcatraz had also kept any water from passing into his lungs, and as the air now began to come back and the reviving oxygen reached his blood, his recovery was amazingly rapid. Before Perris had ceased wondering at the first audible breath the eyes of Alcatraz were lighted with flickering intelligence; then a snort of terror showed that he realized his nearness to the Great Enemy. His very panic acted as a thrillingly powerful restorative. By the time Perris got weakly to his feet, Alcatraz was lunging up the river bank scattering gravel and small rocks behind him.

And Perris made no attempt to throw the rope again. He allowed it to lie limp and wet on the gravel, but turning to watch that magnificent body, shining from the river, he saw the lines of Hervey's hunters coming swinging across the plain, riding to the limit of the speed of their horses.

This was the end, then. In ten minutes, or less, they would be on him, and he without a gun in his hands!

As though he saw the same approaching line of riders, Alcatraz whirled on the edge of the sand, but he did not turn to flee. Instead, he lifted his head and turned his bright eyes on the Great Enemy, and stood there trembling at their nearness! The heart of Perris leaped. A great hope which he dared not frame in thought rushed through his mind, and he stepped slowly forward, his hand extended, his voice caressing. The chestnut winced one step back, and then waited, snorting. There he waited, trembling with fear, chained by curiosity, and ready to leap away in arrowy flight should the sun wink on the tell-tale brightness of steel or the noosed rope dart whispering through the air above him. But there was no such sign of danger. The man came steadily on with his right hand stretched out palm up in the age-old token of amity, and as he approached he kept talking. Strange power was in that voice to enter the ears of the stallion and find a way to his heart of hearts. The fierce and joyous battle-note which he had heard on the day of the great fight was gone and in its place was a fiber of piercing gentleness. It thrilled Alcatraz as the touch of the man's fingers had thrilled him on another day.

Now he was very near, yet Perris did not hurry, did not change the quiet of his words. By the nearness his face was become the dominant thing. What was there between the mountains so terrible and so gentle, so full of awe, of wisdom, and of beauty, as this human face? Behind the eyes the outlaw horse saw the workings of that mystery which had haunted his still evenings in the desert—the mind.

Far away the grey mare was neighing plaintively and the scared cowpony trailed in the distance wondering why these free creatures should come so close to man, the enslaver; but to Alcatraz the herd was no more than a growth of trees; nothing existed under the sky saving that hand ceaselessly outstretched towards him, and the steady murmur of the voice.

He began to wonder: what would happen if he waited until the finger tips were within a hair's-breadth of his nose? Surely there would be no danger, for even if the Great Enemy slid onto his back again he could not stay, weak as Red Perris now was.

Alcatraz winced, but without moving his feet; and when he straightened the finger tips touched the velvet of his nose. He stamped and snorted to frighten the hunter away but the hand moved dauntlessly high and higher—it rested between his eyes—it passed across his head, always with that faint tingle of pleasure trailing behind the touch; and the voice was saying in broken tones: "Some damn fools say they ain't a God! Some damn fools! Something for nothing. That's what He gives! Steady, boy: steady!"

Between perfect fear and perfect pleasure, the stallion shuddered. Now the Great Enemy was beside him with a hand slipping down his neck. Why did he not swerve and race away? What power chained him to the place? He jerked his head about and caught the shoulder of Perris in his teeth. He could crush through muscles and sinews and smash the bone. But the teeth of Alcatraz did not close for the hunter made no sign of fear or pain.

"You're considerable of an idiot, Alcatraz, but you don't know no better," the voice was saying. "That's right, let go that hold. In the old days I'd of had my rope on you quicker'n a wink. But what good in that? The hoss I love ain't a down-headed, mean-hearted man-killer like you used to be; it's the Alcatraz that I've seen running free here in the Valley of the Eagles. And if you come with me, you come free and you stay free. I don't want to set no brand on you. If you stay it's because you like me, boy; and when you want to leave the corral gate will be sure open. Are you coming along?"

The fingers of that gentle hand had tangled in the mane of Alcatraz, drawing him softly forward. He braced his feet, snorting, his ears back. Instantly the pressure on his mane ceased. Alcatraz stepped forward.

"By God," breathed the man. "It's true! Alcatraz, old hoss, d'you think I'd ever of tried to make a slave out of you if I'd guessed that I could make you a partner?"

Behind them, the rattle of volleying hoofs was sweeping closer. The rain had ceased. The air was a perfect calm, and the very grunt of the racing horses was faintly audible and the cursing of the men as they urged their mounts forward. Towards that approaching fear, Alcatraz turned his head. They came as though they would run him into the river. But what did it all mean? So long as one man stood beside him, he was shielded from the enmity of all other men. That had been true even in the regime of the dastardly Cordova.

"Steady!" gasped Red Perris. "They're coming like bullets, Alcatraz, old timer! Steady!"

One hand rested on the withers, the other on the back of the chestnut, and he raised himself gingerly up. Under the weight the stallion shrank catwise, aside and down. But there was no wrench of a curb in his mouth, no biting of the cinches. In the old days of his colthood, a barelegged boy used to come into the pasture and jump on his bare back. His mind flashed back to that—the bare, brown legs. That was before he had learned that men ride with leather and steel. He waited, holding himself strongly on leash, ready to turn loose his whole assortment of tricks—but Perris slipped into place almost as lightly as that dimly remembered boy in the pasture.

To the side, that line of rushing riders was yelling and waving hats. And now the light winked and glimmered on naked guns.

"Go!" whispered Perris at his ear. "Alcatraz!"

And the flat of his hand slapped the stallion on the flank. Was not that the old signal out of the pasture days, calling for a gallop?

He started into a swinging canter. And a faint, half-choked cry of pleasure from the lips of his rider tingled in his ears. For your born horseman reads his horse by the first buoyant moment, and what Red Jim Perris read of the stallion surpassed his fondest dreams. A yell of wonder rose from Hervey and his charging troop. They had seen Red Jim come battered and exhausted from his struggle with the stallion the day before, and now he sat upon the bareback of the chestnut—a miracle!

"Shoot!" yelled Hervey. "Shoot for the man. You can't hit the damned hoss!"

In answer, a volley blazed, but what they had seen was too much for the nerves of even those hardy hunters and expert shots. The volley sang about the ears of Perris, but he was unscathed, while he felt Alcatraz gather beneath him and sweep into a racing pace, his ears flat, his neck extended. For he knew the meaning of that crashing fire. Fool that he had been not to guess. He who had battled with him the day before, but battled without man's ordinary tools of torture; he who had saved him this very day from certain death in the water; this fellow of the flaming red hair, was in truth so different from other men, that they hunted him, they hated him, and therefore they were sending their waspish and invisible messengers of death after him. For his own safety, for the life of the man on his back, Alcatraz gave up his full speed.

And Perris bowed low along the stallion's neck and cheered him on. It was incredible, this thing that was happening. They had reached top speed, and yet the speed still increased. The chestnut seemed to settle towards the earth as his stride lengthened. He was not galloping. He was pouring himself over the ground with an endless succession of smooth impulses. The wind of that running became a gale. The blown mane of Alcatraz whipped and cut at the face of Perris, and still the chestnut drove swifter and swifter.

He was cutting down the bank of the river which had nearly seen his death a few moments before, striving to slip past the left flank of Hervey's men, and now the foreman, yelling his orders, changed his line of battle, and the cowpunchers swung to the left to drive Alcatraz into the very river. The change of direction unsettled their aim. It is hard at best to shoot from the back of a running horse at an object in swift motion; it is next to impossible when sharp orders are being rattled forth. They fired as they galloped, but their shots flew wild.

In the meantime, they were closing the gap between them and the river bank to shut off Alcatraz, but for every foot they covered the chestnut covered two, it seemed. He drove like a red lightning bolt, with the rider flattened on his back, shaking his fist back at the pursuers.

"Pull up!" shouted Lew Hervey, in sudden realization that Alcatraz would slip through the trap. "Pull up! And shoot for Perris! Pull up!"

They obeyed, wrenching their horses to a halt, and as they drew them up, Red Jim, with a yell of triumph, straightened on the back of the flying horse and waved back to them. The next instant his shout of defiance was cut short by the bark of three rifles, as Hervey and Shorty and Little Joe, having halted their horses, pitched their guns to their shoulders and let blaze after the fugitive. There was a sting along the shoulder of Perris as though a red hot knife had slashed him; a bullet had grazed the skin.

Ah, but they would have a hard target to strike, from now on! The trick which Alcatraz had learned in his own flights from the hunters he now brought back into play. He began to swerve from side to side as he raced.

Another volley roared from the cursing cowpunchers behind them, but every bullet flew wide as the chestnut swerved.

"Damn him!" yelled Lew Hervey. "Has the hoss put the charm on the hide of that skunk, too?"

For in the fleeing form of Red Perris he saw all his hopes eluding his grasp. With Red Jim escaped and his promise to the rancher unfulfilled, what would become of his permanent hold on Oliver Jordan? Ay, and Red Jim, once more in safety and mounted on that matchless horse, would swoop down on the Valley of the Eagles and strike to kill, again, again, and again!

No wonder there was an agony shrill in the voice of the foreman as he shouted: "Once more!"

Up went the shining barrels of the rifles, followed the swerving form of the horseman for a moment, and then, steadied to straight, gleaming lines, they fired at the same instant, as though in obedience to an unspoken order.

And the form of Red Perris was knocked forward on the back of Alcatraz!

Some place in his body one of those bullets had struck. They saw him slide far to one side. They saw, while they shouted in triumph, that Alcatraz instinctively shortened his pace to keep his slipping burden from falling.

"He's done!" yelled Hervey, and shoving his rifle back in its holster, he spurred again in the pursuit.

But Red Perris was not done. Scrambling with his legs, tugging with his arms, he drew himself into position and straightway collapsed along the back of Alcatraz with both hands interwoven in the mane of the horse.

And the stallion endured it! A shout of amazement burst from the foreman and his men. Alcatraz had tossed up his head, sent a ringing neigh of defiance floating behind him, and then struck again into his matchless, smooth flowing gallop!

Perhaps it was not so astonishing, after all, as some men could have testified who have seen horses that are devils under spur and saddle become lambs when the steel and the leather they have learned to dread are cast away.

But all Alcatraz could understand, as his mind grasped vaguely towards the meaning of the strange affair, was that the strong, agile power on his back had been suddenly destroyed. Red Perris was now a limp and hanging weight, something no longer to be feared, something to be treated, at will, with contempt. The very voice was changed and husky as it called to him, close to his ear. And he no longer dared to dodge, because at every swerve that limp burden slid far to one side and dragged itself back with groans of agony. Then something warm trickled down over his shoulder. He turned his head. From the breast of the rider a crimson trickle was running down over the chestnut hair, and it was blood. With the horror of it he shuddered.

He must gallop gently, now, at a sufficient distance to keep the rifles from speaking behind him, but slowly and softly enough to keep the rider in his place. He swung towards the mares, running, frightened by the turmoil, in the distance. But a hand on his neck pressed him back in a different direction and down into the trail which led, eventually, to the ranch of Oliver Jordan. Let it be, then, as the man wished. He had known how to save a horse from the Little Smoky. He would be wise enough to keep them both safe even from other men, and so, along the trail towards the ranch, the chestnut ran with a gait as gentle as the swing and light fall of a ground swell in mid-ocean.

CHAPTER XXVII
THE END OF THE RACE

FAR behind him he could see the pursuers driving their horses at a killing gallop. He answered their spurt and held them safely in the distance with the very slightest of efforts. All his care was given to picking out the easiest way, and avoiding jutting rocks and sharp turns which might unsettle the rider. Just as, in those dim old days in the pasture, when the short brown legs of the boy could not encompass him enough to gain a secure grip, he used to halt gently, and turn gently, for fear of unseating the urchin. How far more cautious was his maneuvering now! Here on his back was the power which had saved him from the river. Here on his back was he whose trailing fingers had given him his first caress.

He had no power of reason in his poor blind brain to teach him the why and the wherefore. But he had that overmastering impulse which lives in every gentle-blooded horse—the great desire to serve. A mustang would have been incapable of such a thing, but in Alcatraz flowed the pure strain of the thoroughbred, tracing back to the old desert stock where the horse lives in the tent of his master, the most cherished member of the family. There was in him dim knowledge of events through which he himself had never passed. By the very lines of his blood there was bred in him a need for human affection and human care, just as there was bred in him the keen heart of the racer. And now he knew to the full that exquisite delight of service with the very life of a helpless man given into his keeping.

One ear he canted back to the pain-roughened voice which spoke at his ear. The voice was growing weaker and weaker, just as the grip of the legs was decreasing, and the hands were tangled less firmly in his mane, but now the bright-colored buildings of the ranch appeared through the trees. They were passing between the deadly rows of barbed wire with far-off mutter of the pursuing horses beating at his ear and telling him that all escape was cut off. Yet still the man held him to the way through a mingling of trails thick with the scents of man, of man-ridden horses. The burden on his back now slipped from side to side at every reach of his springy gallop.

They came in sight of the ranch house itself. The failing voice rose for one instant into a hoarse cry of joy. Far behind, rose a triumphant echo of shouting. Yes, the trap was closed, and his only protection from the men riding behind was this half-living creature on his back.

Out from the arched entrance to the patio ran a girl. She started back against the 'dobe wall of the house and threw up one hand as though a miracle had flashed across her vision. Alcatraz brought his canter to a trot that shook the loose body on his back, and then he was walking reluctantly forward, for towards the girl the rider was directing him against all his own power of reason. She was crying out, now, in a shrill voice, and presently through the shadowy arch swung the figure of a big man on crutches, who shouted even as the girl had shouted.

Oliver Jordan, reading through the lines of his foreman's letter, had returned to find out what was going wrong, and from his daughter's tale he had learned more than enough.

Trembling at the nearness of these two human beings, but driven on by the faint voice, and the guiding hands, Alcatraz passed shuddering under the very arch of the patio entrance and so found himself once more—and forever—surrendered into the power of men!

But the weak figure on his back had relaxed, and was sliding down. He saw the gate closing the patio swing to. He saw the girl run with a cry and receive the bleeding body of Red Perris into her arms. He saw the man on crutches swing towards them, exclaiming "—without even a bridle! Marianne, he must have hypnotized that hoss!"

"Oh, Dad," the girl wailed, "if he dies—if he dies——"

The eyes of Perris, where he lay on the flagging, opened wearily.

"I'll live—I can't die! But Alcatraz ... keep him from butcher Hervey ... keep him safe...."

Then his gaze fixed on the face of Oliver Jordan and his eyes widened in amazement.

"My father," she said, as she cut away the shirt to get at the wound.

"Him!" muttered Perris.

"Partner," said Oliver Jordan, wavering above the wounded man on his crutches, "what's done is done."

"Ay," said Perris, smiling weakly, "if you're her father that trail is sure ended. Marianne—get hold of my hand—I'm going out again ... keep Alcatraz safe...."

His eyes closed in a faint.

Between the cook and Marianne they managed to carry the limp figure to the shelter of the arcade just as Hervey and his men thundered up to the closed gate of the patio, and there the foreman drew rein in a cloud of dust and cursed his surprise at the sight of the ranchman.

The group in the patio, and the shining form of Alcatraz, were self explanatory. His plans were ruined at the very verge of a triumph. He hardly needed to hear the voice of Jordan saying: "I asked you to get rid of a gun-fighting killer—and you've tried to murder a *man*. Hervey, get out of the Valley and stay out if you're fond of a whole skin!"

And Hervey went.

* * * * *

There followed a strange time for Alcatraz. He could not be led from the patio. They could only take him by tying every hoof and dragging him, and such force Marianne would not let the cowpunchers use. So day after day he roamed in that strange corral while men came and stared at him through the strong bars of the gate, but no one dared enter the enclosure with the wild horse saving the girl alone, and even she could not touch him.

It was all very strange. And strangest of all was when the girl came out of the door through which the master had been carried and looked at Alcatraz, and wept. Every evening she came but she had no way of answering the anxious whinny with which he called for Red Jim again.

Strange, too, was the hush which brooded over the house. Even the cowpunchers, when they came to the gate, talked softly. But still the master did not come. Two weeks dragged on, weary weeks of waiting, and then the door to the house opened and again they carried him out on a wicker couch, a pale and wasted figure, around whom the man on the crutches and the girl and half a dozen cowpunchers gathered laughing and talking all at once.

"Stand back from him, now," ordered Marianne, "and watch Alcatraz."

So they drew away under the arcade and Alcatraz heard the voice of the master calling weakly.

It was not well that the others should be so near. For how could one tell from what hand a rope might be thrown or in what hand a gun might suddenly flash? But still the voice called and Alcatraz went slowly, snorting his protest and suspicion, until he stood at the foot of the couch and stretching forth his nose, still with his frightened glance fixed on the watchers, Alcatraz sniffed the hand of Red Jim. It turned. It patted him gently. It drew his gaze away from the others and into the eyes of this one man, the mysterious eyes which understood so much.

"A lone trail is right enough for a while, old boy," Red Jim was saying, "but in the end we need partners, a man and a woman and a horse and a man."

And Alcatraz, feeling the trail of the finger tips across the velvet skin of his muzzle, agreed.

THE END.

The Echo Library
www.echo-library.com

Please visit our website to download a complete catalogue of our books. We specialise in out-of-copyright reprints in all subjects. We publish a range of Large Print Editions of classic titles.

Books for re-printing

Suggestions for re-printing can be sent to titles@echo-library.com. Titles must be out-of-copyright or you must own the copyright. They can be in digital or published form.

If we do not wish to add the title to our catalogue then we can reprint for you. Costs depend on the format of the manuscript or book and its size.

Feedback

Because we have no direct contact with our customers we would welcome constructive comments to feedback@echo-library.com

Complaints

If there is a serious error in the text or layout please advise us by sending details to complaints@echo-library.com and we will supply a corrected copy, usually within 15 working days (it may take longer outside the UK and USA).

If there is a printing fault or the book is damaged please refer to your supplier.

Printed in the United States
66786LVS00003B/139